Impeccable

by

Lauren Shiro

Vanilla Heart Publishing
USA

Impeccable
by Lauren Shiro

Published by: Vanilla Heart Publishing
www.VanillaHeartBooksAndAuthors.com
10121 Evergreen Way, 25-156
Everett, WA 98204 USA

ISBN-13: 9780692232521 ISBN-10: 0692232524

10 9 8 7 6 5 4 3 2 Second Edition

First Printing, June 2014
Printed in the United States of America

Impeccable

by

Lauren Shiro

Table of Contents

Dedication

To my mother: for your endless love and support through both the good times and bad. I may never say it enough, but I greatly appreciate all that you do and I love you!

Acknowledgements

To Kimberlee: You are so much more than a publisher. Thank you for believing in me as a writer and a person. You are a tremendous blessing in my life.

To Chelle: I can never thank you enough. You are my editor, my friend, my confidant, and more! You are a terrific person, and I love you more than words can ever say.

Chapter One

The vibration of her Blackberry woke Carol. She slowly opened her very heavy eyes. Everything around her was blurry. She blinked several times and tried to focus her eyes on the number displayed on her Blackberry screen. Squinting, she was able to make out the incoming caller's number. It was a client, a good client, calling with an emergency. It looked like they had already called a few times, but she had somehow missed those previous calls.

Carol sighed, and stood up. Even though she was exhausted and had no interest in working at all, she knew she couldn't ignore this emergency call. They called her directly, so she couldn't send Will out. This was her life, to be at her client's beck and call. Once again she sighed, knowing that she had to leave.

As she took a few steps, she noticed she was off-balance and stumbled. Carol assumed she was more tired than she had initially realized. She paid no attention to the coffee table with the pill vials and empty glass still sitting there, blatantly displaying their culpability. Unable to remember what had transpired just a little while earlier, Carol concentrated on each step as she walked towards the garage.

Slowly, she opened the door to the garage. She stared at the two cars. Her mind was far too foggy to drive the GTO. She didn't have the coordination or wherewithal to handle the stick shift. She hated the idea of using the Camry, but Carol knew it was her only option because of the rain and her weariness.

As soon as she got into the car, Carol was fighting back a flood of memories she and Alex had shared in this car. The Camry was old, but ever so precious to Carol. Carol was so tired and emotional that she forgot to buckle her seatbelt. Hesitating, Carol started to slowly pull out of the garage. She nearly crashed into the garage door when she realized she hadn't hit the button for it to open.

Luckily, Carol was able to stop the car within inches of disaster. Carol tried to take a few deep breaths when she hit the button, hoping to calm herself. While her heart raced from the near accident, she waited for the garage door to open. Once the outside world was completely visible, she drove cautiously towards her client's office.

Even though she was tired, the drive seemed tolerable – at first. It didn't take long, until exhaustion overtook her. The longer she drove, the more unbearable the drive became. Mile after mile, Carol was fighting her tiredness. Her eyelids were heavy and begging to close. She fought to concentrate on the wet, slick road. Carol couldn't keep focused. Her head slumped down and she had to jerk herself awake only to repeat the pattern countless times. She knew she was tired and depressed, but Carol couldn't understand why she was so exhausted.

She fought valiantly to keep her eyes open as she drove, but the weights on her eyelids were far too heavy for Carol. Eventually, her eyes shut and did not open again. Blackness swept over her.

Carol could vaguely hear all kinds of voices and noises. People were shouting all around her, but she was unable to comprehend their words.

Waves of blue and white occasionally flashed in her eyes. Her surroundings were nothing more than swirls of paint and colors. Her eyes were unable to fix themselves on anyone or anything.

Her head felt heavy and flopping all around. Carol never felt so out of control of her own movements. It was a strange feeling, yet she didn't – she couldn't care. Her thoughts were foggy. Carol felt as though she was in a strange dream, and could not wake up.

She couldn't feel her body. She felt nothing, no pain, nothing, no heat, and no cold. She couldn't feel anything. Where was she that she lacked all sensation? Carol diligently tried to focus on her surroundings and tried to make sense of all the activity going on around her, but she was unable to sustain that for long. Once again her eyes rolled back and Carol was consumed by black.

"I have two megs per keg of morphine per hour, doctor." It was a woman's voice.

"Morphine? Doctor, she's unconscious from a head injury. Shouldn't she be given an NSAID or any other form of pain management other than an opiate?"

"Okay, Ronnie. What did they teach you about morphine in school?"

"It raises intracranial pressure and there's the risk of respiratory depression. That's too risky for a patient like this."

"Very good, Ronnie. Normally that's true. She's stable for now though, so it should be fine. If her resps decrease too much, we can always throw her on the ventilator. Now, you are right about the intracranial pressure. So we have to watch for any signs of brain trauma. Now, we need to get her moved into iso as quickly as possible."

"ICU said that they are getting an isolation room ready for her right now. She should be able to transport in about fifteen minutes," the woman said.

Carol took in a deep breath. There was an odd sound to her breathing and she could feel something covering her nose and mouth. She couldn't open her eyes at all. Carol was lost. She had no idea where she was or what was happening. This was the worst nightmare she had ever experienced. Suddenly, she felt a cold shiver run through her body. She tried to curl up for warmth, but she was unable to move. She heard strange noises coming from somewhere behind her.

"Hamm. It seems she has a slight arrhythmia," the first male voice said.

"She's also bradycardic, doctor." Once again, the woman spoke.

"Okay. I want her on Epi, but watch for any PVC's. I want her under constant surveillance, and with her vitals checked q fifteen. You understand?" The first man who was referred to only as "doctor," said.

"Yes," the woman answered.

Carol was confused by their words and her inability to see. She took another deep breath in. Just as she did, her ability to think disappeared and she felt herself get swept away into another deep sleep.

Chapter Two

"Carol? Carol?" Another voice, a woman's, was calling her.

Carol still felt the pressure of something covering her nose and mouth. She could feel a blanket tightly wrapped around her. She used every ounce of strength just to open her eyes. Slowly, her blurry vision cleared as she opened her eyes. There was woman standing over her that Carol did not recognize.

She wanted to know who this stranger was. Carol tried to speak. All that came out was a weak moan.

"There. You're up! Good. It's time for dinner, hon."

Dinner? Dinner! This made no sense. Who the hell was this woman and was it dinnertime already? Carol tried to wrap her head around everything, but she felt as if she were had entered *The Twilight Zone*. Her foggy thoughts succumbed to confusion and anger. Again, Carol grunted.

"Okay, okay," the woman said gently. She sat next to Carol, and carefully removed the mask from Carol's face. She had soft, curly brown hair that just brushed her shoulders. Her eyes were a soft blue-green color. She was wearing a shapeless bio-hazard suit. She wore a surgical mask that loosely hung from her face. Despite the impersonal barrier of her clothing, she had a very kind aura about her. "This is good. Now you can just have a nasal cannula instead of that God awful thing," she said disregarding Carol's grunts. "Now, I am just going to slowly move your bed so that you're sitting upright and then we'll slowly eat some dinner, okay?"

"Uhhhhhh." That was as close as Carol could get to giving this woman any kind of response.

Slowly the bed moved and Carol was sitting up. Tiny forkful by tiny forkful this woman fed Carol.

As she was eating, another woman, also wearing a white biohazard suit, entered the room. "Oh, you're up. That's faster than any of us expected. That's great." She had flowing blonde hair pulled back into a ponytail. Her eyes were as bright as a summer sky. She smiled under her surgical mask as she approached Carol.

"Hi Carol, I'm Shelby. I'll be your charge nurse. I'm here to check your vital signs."

"Shel, also put in for her to be placed on oxygen through a cannula rather than the mask. This way she can eat and talk since she's awake now."

"No problem, Deirdre. I'll get that as soon as I'm done here."

Gently, Shelby checked Carol's pulse, listened to her heart, checked all the monitors and machines, and then left the room all in a matter of mere moments.

She quickly returned and hooked up a length of small plastic tubing to the oxygen supply outlet in Carol's room. The tubing was all too familiar. Carol had seen it far too many times. Now, she was supposed to wear the tubing from those memories.

"No," Carol was just barely able to form the word.

"What was that?" Shelby turned around and looked at Carol. "I'm sorry Carol, I didn't understand you. What did you say?"

"No," her voice squeaked as she spoke.

"You don't want this?" Shelby asked.

"No," Carol said as firmly as possible. She coughed a few times after she spoke.

"I know it's not the most pleasant thing in the world, hon. But you have to."

"No."

"Carol, you need this. You need to be on oxygen. I'm sorry."

"Carol?" This voice was familiar. The tone was gentle and warm even though she was stern when she said her name. Carol rolled her eyes to the side to see Candace standing in the doorway. "Carol, you're really awake!" Candace exclaimed as she ran towards Carol's bed. Candace was also in a strange suit, and she was wearing a mask.

"Yes, she is. She's doing quite well – and quickly too. Though she doesn't want this," Shelby said holding up the nasal cannula.

"Oh," Candace said. "I think I know why. My sister passed away recently and Carol saw her with wearing one like this before she died. I'll bet it's bringing back some bad memories."

"Oh, I'm sorry." Shelby gently replied.

"Uhhhhhh," Carol moaned. Candace was right. Carol hoped that her moan made sense to them.

"I'm so sorry, Carol. That's a terrible thing to go through. I'm sorry that you only know it as a bad thing. It's not really. I still have to put it on you, okay?" Shelby said.

Carol grunted like a Cro-Magnon man.

"I know, sweetie." Candace said as she gently rubbed Carol's arm. "It's okay, Carol. Let this nice woman do what she needs to do, okay?"

Carol growled a displeased groan, but she allowed Shelby to hook up the remainder of the tubing.

"Ladies, would you mind if I had a few moments with Carol, alone?" Candace asked.

"No, not at all." Deirdre answered.

"That's fine. I will be back to check her vitals again in fifteen minutes, though," Shelby replied.

"That would be great. Thank you."

The two women got up and did not leave the room quickly enough for Carol.

"I can't believe you're back with us, Carol." Candace paused before she spoke again. "It's a miracle. God knows Byron, Erin, Tyrone and I have been praying for you like crazy. We even had the church hold a special vigil for you last night.

"We're all so excited that you're alive. We've missed you. We've been worried about you. Even Byron."

"Mmmmmmm," Carol replied.

"I know. He should have called you back. I know that. Trust me, I ripped him a new one for that. Girl, I wasn't going to let that slide! He was blinded by his anger. Now he gets it, though. And he's sorry. He really is. He's on his way now."

"No," Carol weakly mumbled. She started coughing. It was a dry, hacking cough. Once she started, it took Carol a few moments to control it.

"Carol, please just let it go. We're family. He's coming here because he loves you. We all love you."

Carol paused. She had always hoped that the Whetherby family would take her in as one of their own. She was still skeptical, though, after all that had transpired over the years.

Carol slowly lifted a finger and pointed to Candace's suit.

"Carol?" Candace looked at Carol through soft, sympathetic eyes. She was as radiant as ever. She was still extremely pregnant as well.

Carol looked back at the young woman. Her questioning eyes were easy to read.

"You don't know why you're here, do you?" Candace asked softly.

"No," Carol forced the word out.

“Oh, sweetie. You were in an accident – a really bad car accident.” There was a brief silence before Candace spoke again. “Do you remember taking all of those pills at home?”

Carol looked at Candace with a blank expression.

Candace sighed heavily.”You OD’d on your meds, Carol. You tried to kill yourself. But then, you left the house. You must have gotten a phone call or something because you tried to drive. You got into Alex’s car and you drove...” Candace paused. “You crashed into a tree, Carol.”

Carol looked up at Candace suddenly. Candace saw the fear in her eyes.

“No, it’s okay. No one else was hurt.”

Again, Carol fought to lift her finger high enough for Candace to see. She pointed at Candace’s outfit.

“This? Oh, everyone is required to wear this stuff to protect you since you’re an AIDS patient. Your immune system is seriously compromised, they told us that. We don’t want to risk making you sick in any way. Your poor body is going through enough as it is. This is to protect you.”

Carol looked down at her hospital bed in shame.

“Ssssshhhhh. It’s okay, Carol. No one is judging you or is mad at you.” She stopped momentarily before she continued. “Alex’s car is totaled, Carol. But like I said, it’s okay. We don’t mind. We’re not angry. We’re just thankful that you’re still alive.”

Carol slowly gazed back up at Candace and tears rolled down her face.

Byron, Erin, Candace and Tyrone stood around the hospital bed.

“It’s a miracle she’s still here,” Byron whispered to the others through his mask. They all donned the bunny suits and surgical masks.

"It is. The prayers and the service worked," Candace said.

"I just can't believe that she's here – that she's like this. I never knew she was that depressed. I never knew she felt that way. Did any of you?" Erin asked the group. "She didn't even leave a note. Why wouldn't she at least have left a note?"

"My guess is that Carol felt so down about herself, she figured she wasn't good enough to live and there was no reason to say goodbye. She probably assumed no one would even care enough to read it." Candace said. Wisdom flowed from her words despite her young age.

"I still don't get it. Do any of you?" Erin looked around and addressed the group.

Everyone shook their heads.

"Why did she do this? Why does she feel this way?" Erin asked even though she knew no one had an answer.

"Who knows?" Tyrone replied. "It's a shame," he continued. "She's a good person. A really good person. We *all* see that in her. Why can't she see that in herself?" Tyrone asked the family.

"I don't know, T. she never heard us or Alex over the years. Maybe she still can't hear us now," Byron responded.

"I can hear you," Carol slowly spat out the words. Her voice was scratchy and she coughed a few times.

"I'm sorry, Carol." Erin started.

"No, s'okay." Carol's voice was weak and it was obvious she had to force every letter out.

"Do you want us to leave?" Tyrone asked Carol.

"No." Carol stared blankly at the ceiling. She couldn't move her head to speak to anyone directly.

"What do you want?" Byron asked in an incredibly soft and caring tone.

"I want my Alex back." Again, Carol coughed.

The group all looked at each other helplessly.

"I know, Carol." Candace responded quickly. "We all do. But she is in a better place now."

"Why the hell aren't I?" Carol croaked through a small coughing fit.

"Carol, I know this difficult. I don't have all the answers. None of us do. All we can tell you is that there is some reason why you're still here," Candace replied.

"That's bull. I hate it. Why can't I just die? I don't want to do this any more." As weak as she was, Carol's anger was incredibly strong, and extremely obvious.

"Shhhhh," Erin quietly whispered in Carol's ear. "It's okay."

"No, Erin, it's not okay. Alex is gone and I am fucking stuck here!"

"Maybe God..." Candace started.

"God? There is no God!" Carol said callously. Once again, Carol had another coughing spell.

"Carol, aren't you afraid of death? You're too young to be here – especially under these circumstances," Byron said gently.

"I'm not afraid of death. I long for it." Carol snapped back.

"Maybe we should go." Tyrone said.

"I hate to leave her," Candace quietly said to him.

"I know. I do too. But she's hurting – bad. I don't know if there's anything any of us can say that will help right now, baby." Tyrone replied.

While the four visitors quietly whispered among themselves, Shelby returned to Carol's room.

"Hi guys," she said brightly.

She was answered with various greetings.

"I hate to kick you guys out, but it's time for Carol's next dose of medications. She's going to end up sleeping for quite a while from these."

"That's fine, Shelby." Candace spoke. "Carol's getting a bit agitated anyway. I'm sure she's in a lot of pain and stressed right now. We don't want to make it worse. We'll just let her rest. We'll come back tomorrow."

Carol did her best to shoot Candace an angry look.

"That sounds good. Thanks for visiting."

As the Whetherby family began to leave, Byron pulled Shelby aside. "Shelby, why is Carol coughing so much?" Although Byron whispered, his concern was quite audible.

"Probably from her trache tube. We needed to intubate her to help her breathing. In emergency cases, the tracheal tube can cause irritation. We see it all the time. Patients tell us it's more annoying than anything. She's not sick, that much I can promise you. It's just an annoyance, really. It will take a little while for it to go away, but she's fine."

"Oh, okay." Byron sighed from relief. "Thank you."

"You're more than welcome," she replied in a louder voice. "You all have a good night. I'll see ya tomorrow," Shelby said.

Everyone said good night to Carol and left the room.

"Finally," she mumbled.

"Are you okay, Carol?" Shelby asked.

"Yeah. Just put me to sleep, okay?"

"Okay. Get some good rest. You need it. You have a lot of healing to do," Shelby said as she gently pushed various medications through Carol's multiple IV lines.

Within moments, Carol's anger dissipated and she drifted off to sleep.

Chapter Three

"Good morning, Carol. It's been just over a week now and you're healing fairly well, all things considered." Dr. Ramone said.

"It's been more than a week?" Carol asked in shock. "How long was I unconscious, Dr. Ramone?"

"Three days." He answered quickly.

Carol was stunned by what she heard. Three days? How on Earth had she literally lost three days of her life? It seemed crazy to think that she had been in this hospital for a week. She had no idea that much time had already passed.

"Now, we have to go over your injuries. You're pretty badly beaten up. You're going to need multiple surgeries, which is tricky since you have AIDS."

"Mul, multiple surgeries?" Carol's voice became scratchy, and she forcefully cleared her throat.

"Yes, I'm sorry to say. The worst part is, every time you go under anesthesia, your immune system is suppressed. As an AIDS patient, that presents a number of risks. You need these surgeries without a doubt, but it's going to take a while.

"Here's what we've got: you have 4 fractured ribs; you have a compound fracture of your right femur; you will need pins in both of your legs. You have some superficial wounds to your face from glass and a tree branch, but I'm not overly concerned about those. We might even be able to suture those up just under a local.

"You've already had one surgery: you sliced your femoral artery, so we had to go in and fix it before you bled out. So far, your test results show that the internal bleeding has stopped.

You're extremely bruised, though, so we need to check you for any signs of internal bleeding twice daily. Right now, it doesn't look good overall, but I'm going to wait and see how your body does on its own. It's the best course of action taking everything into account."

"Wait, what? I don't understand."

"I'm sorry Carol. I know this is all rather confusing since we're always all suited up around you and you haven't been able to see much of anything.

"You have casts on both of your legs and special bandaging for your pelvis. You also have a Foley catheter in place."

"A Foley catheter?" Carol's scratchy voiced asked in utter confusion.

"It's a urinary catheter, Carol. You also have a colostomy bag, which..."

"A colostomy bag?" Carol's eyes were wide with fear.

"You need it, at least for right now. It's only a temporary set-up, so it can and will be reversed when the time is right. Don't worry.

"Moving on, your torso is wrapped up because of your fractured ribs. You are also wearing a neck brace.

"Again, your superficial wounds aren't too bad. They should heal on their own.

"Regardless, all of this will take a while since you are an AIDS patient. Only time will tell. Just be prepared to be in here for a long time.

"With each of these surgeries come great risk and a significant healing period because of your immune system. I will admit that I am very tentative about these surgeries. For now, we are going to take things one day at a time. Your blood work will be monitored frequently. As time progresses, your medication regimen will probably change and we will see about the surgeries depending on how quickly you bounce back from all this."

"I'm going to be honest with you, Carol. I'm really quite concerned here. You have a history of some mild liver issues. You did a real number on your liver by taking all of those medications. It's a lot for a normal liver to process, let alone a weak one. And that's not to mention the toll this has taken on the rest of your body. This is going to be quite intensive, extensive and painful. The road to recovery is not an easy one in this case."

Carol just stared back at the ceiling. She had only met this man and hadn't even seen his face. Yet here he stood telling her what her future was going to look like. Carol sighed as deeply as she could, though she was limited by her pain and bandages. She even failed at ending her own life. Carol truly could not do anything right. She never hated herself more than she did at that very moment.

"They said I need multiple surgeries, Will," Carol spoke softly.

"I'm sorry, Carol. I really am. What kind of prognosis are they giving you?" Will was looking down at her with tremendous sympathy in his dark brown eyes.

"Guarded. They think I'll eventually pull through, but they said it's gonna be a long time." Carol coughed a few times.

"Shit. I'm so sorry. I really am."

"So am I, Will. I couldn't even fucking do this right," Carol said dejectedly.

"Carol, I am not going there with you. Understand? Shit. Girl you got more talent in that tiny ass little pinky of yours. You've got to stop with this, okay?"

"What does it matter, Will? Alex is gone."

Will hesitated before he spoke. He hated to seem insensitive, but he thought Carol needed some tough love. "Yeah, that's right." He said harshly. "Alex is gone. It sucks. We all miss her like hell. But that doesn't mean we all should stop living."

"I didn't think you'd understand."

"Carol, I *do* understand. I get it. I know I'd be fucking lost without Robyn. But damn it, I'm still going to keep on living if she goes first. I'd have no other choice but to keep going."

Carol lay silently in her bed while her best friend sat next to her in his bunny suit and trying to comfort her. She still couldn't move to look at him. She had only been in this hospital for eight days and she already had the ceiling completely memorized.

"Look, Carol." Will started. "I know this is hard as hell on you. I know. I've known you too long and I've seen you go through a lot of shit. But damn it, Carol. You're stronger than this. You're better than this. You have to move on."

"How do you move on when you've killed the love of your life?" Carol's tone was cynical and depressed.

"You did not kill Alex and you know it! You have got to stop blaming yourself for everything. Damn it!" Will turned away, trying to ignore his frustration and anger.

"How is everything at Dawson? You holding up okay?" Carol asked, she just wanted to change the conversation with Will. He didn't understand her or her feelings. She'd rather just keep them to herself.

Will sighed heavily. "Good. Everyone's asking about you, praying for you and all that. But man, it is crazy. I am having one hell of a time keeping up with all the calls and all the other shit. Robyn's been helping me out with all the paperwork. How'd you handle it?"

"I was never doing it solo, Will."

“It’s great that the business hasn’t been hit too hard with the economy and all, but I’m dying. I’m up early tackling all the field service calls, getting to the office late trying to keep up with inventory, paperwork, taxes... I’m hardly sleeping. Sorry. I don’t mean to complain when...”

“It’s fine, Will. Listen, I think I may have an answer for you. Go through my Blackberry and find the number for Nate Adams. I met him in our support group. He’s a damn good guy, Will. Hire him. He’ll help you. He’ll be a good addition to Dawson.” Again, Carol coughed a few times before she was able to clear her throat.

“Nate Adams? Okay. You sure you want to do this?”

“Yes. Just get his number and call him. Tell him I told you to call.”

“Okay, boss. Whatever you say.”

Another day in the hospital was quickly coming to a close. Carol had been visited by everyone in the family just as she had been every day before. She was tired, painful and simply miserable in this horrendous existence.

Candace stayed with her until everyone else was gone. She made small talk for a while which only annoyed Carol further. Finally, as the glow from the setting sun came through the window, Candace said what had been on her mind all day.

“Carol, i’ve been doing some thinking.”

“Okay great, here it comes,” Carol mumbled under her breath.

“I’m worried about you. You’re obviously very depressed, but you’ve never said anything to anyone all these years. You had no way of expressing your feelings and look at what happened! It’s not healthy to keep these things bottled up, Carol.”

Carol sighed a cynical sigh.

"Look, I brought this for you. Here. It's a journal." Candace spoke softly as she handed Carol a small black book.

"Thanks," Carol said sarcastically.

"Carol, please." Candace begged.

Carol paused and took as deep a breath as she could manage. "Okay, i'll use it. I promise, Candace. Can I just be left to sleep now?"

"Sure Carol. I'll see you tomorrow. I love you."

"Yeah." Carol couldn't even say the words. She did love Candace. However, she was unable to express any emotions. For her to speak meaningless and insincere words was worse than saying nothing. Love had no meaning now that Alex was gone.

Chapter 4

Carol could just make out the clock on the wall from the glow of a street light coming through her window. It was after two o'clock in the morning. Her pain was excruciating. She called for a nurse.

No one came into her room. She pressed the call button again. Still no one came. Once again, Carol hit the call button. She waited in eerie silence.

The journal Candace had given her yesterday rested on the small table by her side. Carol could feel its presence and wondered why Candace felt the need to give her something so useless. Carol thought it was a pointless gift, but she had promised Candace she'd use it. Carol debated whether or not she should hold true to her word since promises always seemed empty anyway. After much deliberation, she figured that Candace would never see the book anyway. She didn't have to write if she didn't want to. But, Candace was family. Candace had never broken a promise to her. Despite her reluctance to write, Carol still felt obligated to Candace. She sighed as she quarreled with herself.

Still no signs of a nurse.

"Oh, what the hell?" Carol said to herself. She cautiously reached her arm out and grabbed the book. With no plan, she opened the book to the first blank page.

"Dear -." Carol immediately stopped. Dear whom? Dear Journal? That sounded pretty stupid. How was she to do this if she didn't even take it seriously? Carol tried to think. Carol had no one to write to, no one to address. The only person she wanted to communicate with was Alex.

Alex. She'd love to be able to talk to Alex again. Tears found their way down Carol's cheeks. After a few moments Carol thought maybe she could use the journal to write letters to Alex. With that in mind, Carol started again.

Dear Alex, I feel pretty stupid writing in this book, but Candace gave it to me and I promised her I'd use it.

She paused and concentrated on a picture of Alex she had in her mind.

I'm in the hospital, Alex. I took a shitload of our meds, but it didn't work. I drove your car all messed up from the meds and crashed into a tree. I didn't mean to drive or mess up your car, I should have died, but I didn't. Somehow I fucking survived both. That's not right. I don't get it.

Why am I still here and you're not? There is no life for me without you. This is all so pointless. Another tear wound down her face.

Finally, a nurse, suited up and masked, entered Carol's room. Carol slammed the book shut and tossed it back onto the table.

"Everything okay, Miss Mathers?"

"Uhhh... No. Can I have some more pain medication? This is really unbearable." Carol coughed for several moments.

"Sure."

The suited woman went over to Carol's IV lines and slowly pushed the clear liquid morphine into her vein. Within moments, Carol's pain eased and she fell back to sleep.

There was a deafening crash all around Carol, yet she saw nothing. It seemed as if the sound of glass breaking could be heard for miles. Carol was thrown forward, her chest hit something hard and unforgiving. Her neck was whipped forward and her face fell into something. It was soft, but the impact was so strong that she could feel bones in her face breaking. Just as her head was thrown backwards again, a sharp object sliced her right cheek. Carol still could not see what was going on around her. All she heard was complete chaos.

The world that surrounded her was dark and blurry. She was desperate to figure out where she was, but everything was upside-down and hazy. From the distance, Carol could hear voices, male voices, shouting as they approached.

"Traffic cop called it in."

"She's lucky."

Carol painfully rolled her head to the side to see who these men were. All she could see were indistinct images. The men were blurry blobs as they approached Carol. Slowly, their faces became clearer.

"I've got severe bleeding. Looks like superficial wounds to her face and neck. There's glass everywhere. She's got a pretty sizeable laceration on her face: right side, just under her eye.

"There's significant bruising on her chest. Probable cracked ribs, she hit the steering wheel." This first man had a large, round face. He had light brown hair that fell into his eyes, which were a soft brown color. His voice sounded kind and compassionate.

"She's shocky. BP is sixty six over forty and dropping. Her breathing is ragged. We need to intubate." This man had thick, curly black hair and a fat black moustache. His eyes were dark, but tender. His face came and went within her vision in a heartbeat.

Carol saw a wave of blue and suddenly a tube was being jammed down her throat. She could feel it, but she couldn't move or speak.

"Heart rate has dropped to forty. We've got to move." The first man spoke again.

"Shit! You got the board?"

"Yeah."

"Let me just collar her."

Carol tried to groan. Collar? What kind of collar? Why did these men want to put a collar on her? She didn't want a collar. Carol didn't understand what was going on. Though she tried, she could not make a sound. She screamed as loud as she could in her mind, but not a peep escaped her lips. She tried to move – to do anything to show them that she was awake and aware of what was going on. Yet, her body remained still. The men didn't see that she was awake. Repeatedly Carol tried to make some kind of noise to stop them, but it was to no avail.

Suddenly, there were large hands all around her. She looked around and saw that she was floating in a sea of hands. It was strange – like a surrealist painting. But, these hands were moving. She could feel that they were strong as they held her tightly.

"One... two... three." All at once, all of the hands lifted Carol up. She was surrounded by white now. What was this? What was going on? Carol was petrified. She was laying on something cold and stiff. She was unable to move at all.

"Okay, she's all strapped in," a new voice said.

The wind suddenly picked up. Carol was in a whirlwind; a tornado. She must be in the middle of a tornado. All she could hear were loud noises and this bizarre, extreme wind. Swirls of blue danced in front of her eyes. More colors began swirling into the psychedelic vision, creating new patterns. Carol felt as though she was falling endlessly into this giant kaleidoscope.

Suddenly, she felt as though she had been pushed from the side. Carol's vision changed, and she was now looking up at a young, handsome man with bright blonde hair and crisp blue eyes.

"Thank God you're here." The first man said. "She's really shocky. Her femoral artery has been cut. We have pressure bandaging and the bleeding seems controlled for now.

"We have her on high flow O2 at 15 LPM."

"Okay, they're waiting for us. We'll get her there ASAP."

"Thanks. Good luck," the first man said.

The wind was gone, but loud noises still surrounded Carol. The young man's face disappeared and reappeared sporadically for an indefinite period of time. No one, not even the young man, spoke to her, but there were various voices talking all around her. Carol struggled to hear their words. Nothing they said was making any sense.

A flood of white swept over Carol again. Carol squinted from the brightness of the white wash. There were shadows in the distance that contrasted brightly against the white background. Carol heard beeps and chimes and various indistinguishable noises.

"What do you want me to use?" A new voice spoke. Carol turned her head in the direction she heard the voice coming from. She saw a small blur of green scurry past her and then everything was white once more.

"She's already intubated and on the ventilator. We've got to watch her heart rate closely. She has atropine and epi already. We'll give her some Glyco if she stabilizes in a bit.

"Has anyone gotten the blood results back yet?" A deep male voice spoke.

"Yes, doctor. Here are her blood gases, the cbc, chem, BG and look at this." A female voice spoke.

"Holy shit. Look at this tox panel. This is insane. She's lucky to have any pulse at all. Get the nasogastric tube and suction." Suddenly, a new face appeared and disappeared quickly. It was a man with sharp features and cold grey eyes.

His face left Carol's sight so rapidly, she instantly forgot it.

"Right here," another woman's voice said.

"Okay, let's see what we can suction out." The dark, deep voice said.

There were strange sounds all around, it was impossible to make out anything. Green globules in the shape of people floated all around Carol in a strange but perfectly choreographed dance. Carol tried to focus her sight on any of these green people, but their movements were swift and erratic. She felt nothing but confused.

After a few minutes, the deep-voiced man spoke. "Okay, that seems to be about it. Do we have the tube and the activated charcoal?"

"Yes, doctor."

"Then let's not wait anymore. Pass it and get that in her now." The deep voice sounded rushed.

Another tube, much larger this time. was shoved into Carol's mouth. It hurt just as much as the other one. Her jaw felt like it was being stretched in ways she never imagined possible. She was desperate to get all of this tubing and weird equipment off of her face, but she was unable to move. She couldn't defend herself. Various faces came and went within her vision quickly. No two faces were the same as they bopped all around her.

"Okay. Activated charcoal went down without any difficulties."

"Good. Let's keep an eye on her. I want anticholinergics on hand at all times, as well as epi. God knows she'll wake up in severe pain as well. Let's get her on some morphine. When vomits the activated charcoal back up, we'll just give her more. Meanwhile keep suction ready." The man with the deep voice said.

"Okay. I started morphine k20, doctor." A woman said.

Her face appeared. She had large, kind green eyes. Strands of brown hair peeked out from under a blue hair covering. Her face was worn but kind. She was all Carol could see.

"Morphine? Doctor, she's unconscious. Shouldn't she be given an NSAID or any other form of pain management instead of an opiate?" A new male voice spoke.

"Jesus, Ronnie! What the hell is wrong with you? First you want to knock her down with Etom, now you don't want her to get morphine. Did you graduate last in your class?"

"Damn it! She's stable for now – not as shocky. We have to watch for any signs of brain trauma, though, and then get her moved into ISO after this as quickly as possible."

"ICU said that they are getting an isolation room ready for her right now. She should be able to move as soon as we're done," the woman said. She turned away and disappeared from Carol's sight.

Carol took in a deep breath. As she did, black consumed everything. Carol could no longer see. There was an odd sound to her breathing and she could feel something covering her nose and mouth. She tried, but her eyes were unable to open at all. Carol was still lost. She had no idea where she was or what was happening. This was the worst nightmare she had ever experienced.

Suddenly, she felt a cold shiver run through her body. She tried to curl up for heat, but she was unable to move. She heard strange noises coming from somewhere behind her.

"Hamm. It seems she has a slight arrhythmia," another male voice said.

"She's still bradycardic, doctor. They said she dropped down to forty BPMs on site. She's at fifty six right now. We need to bring her back up." The woman from a few minutes earlier spoke.

"Okay. I want her on epi, but watch for any PVC's."

Carol suddenly felt as if the room was spinning. She was completely disoriented now, and she couldn't see. She again tried screaming for help, but she still couldn't. She desperately wanted – needed – help. Her cries for help weren't even as loud as a squeak. Carol felt her breath escaping her. *Help, somebody, please help*! Carol fought and gasped for air.

As Carol took in a sudden, giant gasp of air, her eyes shot open. Panicked, she looked all around her. She was in her hospital bed as alarms were going off. The setting was familiar, but she still felt a tremendous weight on her chest. She continued to struggle for breath.

A small woman of African descent ran into her room.

"It's okay, Carol." She said. "You must have had a nightmare. You're heart rate is up and some of your other vitals are shaky." This woman's tone was calm and soothing. "I am just going to give you these medicines, and you'll be fine. You just need to relax."

Carol gently rocked side to side in her hospital bed.

"Sssshhhh," the woman comforted her.

Carol felt warmth flowing into her veins.

"It's okay. Lay back down," the woman said gently as she eased Carol back down on her bed. "Close your eyes. You're okay. Just get some rest."

Dear Alex, I'm lying here in solitude. I wish I knew what was going on in the world around me. I hear noises and people talking, but nothing is clear. It's as if everyone wants to hide things from me. It sure makes an insecure girl even more insecure.

I wonder what people think of me. Do they judge me? Do they hate me? Do they pity me or do they simply tolerate me?

Carol closed her eyes for a second and then opened them

again. *What about you, babe? What do you think of me*?

Carol was lying in her bed, staring at the ceiling as usual. She tried to imagine some kind of interesting patterns or designs on the ceiling tiles, but her boredom and depression still won.

Shelby walked into the room, cheerful as ever. "Well I have some good news for you, Miss Carol. We're putting you in a soft brace so you can move your head around a little bit more. This way you're not just staring at that ugly ceiling. You still need to be careful with your neck, but you can look out the window or even at us without being moved or lifting up your bed. Isn't that great?"

"Yeah," Carol said sarcastically.

Another nurse walked into the room. Carol didn't recognize her. It was hard to get to know people's faces because of the precautionary gear they wore in her room.

"Oh good, you're here. If you can just help me do this quickly, you can get back to what you were doing."

"Okay," the woman replied.

Shelby stood on one side of Carol and the other woman went to the other side.

"On my count. One... two... three... lift." Shelby directed. Both women gently raised Carol's head. The unknown women held her head steady as Shelby took off the hard, plastic brace and placed a soft, cushiony foam brace on. Shelby then held Carol's head just like the other woman was holding her.

"How does that feel, Carol?" Shelby asked.

"Fine, I guess." Carol responded. She didn't notice any difference, really, her neck still felt stiff. She wanted to appease Shelby so she would leave and she could return to her solitude. She hoped her answer would do just that.

"Okay. Now we're going to lay you back gently."

The two women slowly and carefully rested Carol's head back on her pillow.

"There," Shelby said brightly as Carol lay back on the pillows. "Now, don't go moving your head around too much. Even what we just did might be a bit much for you. You might be a little sore. So, take it easy and move slowly and carefully. Okay?"

"Okay." Carol answered. She coughed a few times, but was finally able to stop herself.

"Thanks, Janet." Shelby whispered to the other woman as she left. "Alright, Carol. You rest and take it easy. I will see you later, okay?"

"Yeah," Carol feigned a smile. After a moment, Shelby left the room.

Ever so cautiously and hesitantly, Carol slowly turned her head to look out the window. It was already dark. Another day in this hospital had come and gone. The darkness made Carol even more depressed than the ceiling tiles had.

Dear Alex, I totaled your car. Did I tell you that already? I totaled your car. I'm so sorry. I didn't mean to. I was so hazy from all the drugs. I knew I couldn't drive the GTO. I wish I had, though. I didn't want to ruin your car.

I wish I had never woken up after taking those pills. As usual, I just keep fucking everything up. I'm sorry, baby. I really am. I miss you like hell. There's nothing left to say other than: I'm sorry, I miss you and I love you. Love, Carol.

Carol placed the journal back on the small table next to her bed and sighed heavily. Not dying from the over-dose or the accident was a hell far greater than death itself.

Chapter 5

The snow swirled around like a tornado against the grey and dismal background. Carol sighed heavily as she looked out the window. How she wished the snow was indeed a tornado. Then she could be whisked away never to return to her wretched life.

Carol's dark thoughts were interrupted when a man walked into her room. She turned over to see him. He was tall; his Tyvek bunny suit barely fit his lanky limbs. His hair was dark brown, as were his eyes. She looked as deeply as she could into his eyes to see any compassion, but these were shallow and unemotional eyes that rested just above his surgical mask. He sat in a chair opposite Carol's bed.

"Good morning, Carol. My name is Dr. Parker. I am the head of psychiatry here."

"Psychiatry?" Carol's tone reflected her shock and disgust at his presence.

"Yes, Carol. You tried to cause harm to yourself. It is my job to visit with you regularly and to help you work through the issues that brought you to that point.

"Normally, you would be staying in another wing, our in-patient mental health unit, but because of your health status, you need to stay here. We often do group activities, one-on-one time, group therapy sessions and more. Because of the severity of your condition we'll just be doing some daily one-on-one time. But I think you'll find this will be a big help to you."

"Great." Carol said sarcastically.

"When your condition improves and we can move you,

you can join the rest of the unit later on." He tried to sound reassuring. "For now, why don't you tell me what happened?"

Carol stared defiantly at the man. "You come into my room and expect me to tell you about my life? Fuck you! Get out." She hacked her dry cough a few times.

"Carol, I need to evaluate you."

"You can shove that evaluation right up your ass. I said get out!"

They stared at each other in an awkward tension. Carol refused to let this man to win this fight. She'd stare him down as long as it took until he left. The anger in her eyes was undeniable.

Finally after several minutes, Dr. Parker rose. When you feel up to it, I can come back and we can talk."

"Fuck you and your evaluations. I don't need your shit," Carol said.

He nodded gently. "I'll see you again." He turned and left the room.

She slowly turned her head back to gaze at the snow tornado once more.

Candace hesitantly walked into Carol's darkened room. "Hey Carol," she said quietly.

"Hi," Carol weakly replied. Her eyes were still glued to the snow that danced outside her window.

"What's going on, Carol?" Candace slowly sat down in the chair. She was growing increasingly pregnant with each visit.

"Not much. They sent the hospital shrink this morning." Carol didn't turn her attention away from the grey and white world outside her window.

"Oh really? How did that go?"

"I told him to fuck off and he left." Carol said matter-of-factly.

"Carol, I can't believe you did that. That's not like you. What is going on?"

"Nothing, Candace. I just don't want to be bothered. I hate the fact that I'm still here and I would rather just be alone. Hopefully I'll wither away into nothing." Carol cleared her throat. The tracheal irritation never seemed to go away.

"Carol, you don't mean that."

"Yes I do, Candace. I'm sick of it all. Life has nothing to offer me anymore. Everything I ever wanted or needed died when Alex died." Tears silently escaped Carol's eyes.

"We all lost something great when Alex passed, Carol. Byron, Erin, Tyron and I are all still hurting too. You don't just get over something like this. But you won't hear any of us talking like that."

"I don't hear any of you talking period." Carol snapped.

"Carol..." Candace sighed out Carol's name, unsure of what she should say. "Why didn't you talk to the psychiatrist? I really think you should. He'd help you." She replied sympathetically.

"Of course you'd say that! You're on his side."

"On his side? What does that mean?"

"You're just like him, C. And you know it."

"Why? Because I'm a social worker?"

"Whatever. You're all the same. It's my life. If I want to keep it private, then it's staying private."

"Carol, please. You need this."

Carol slowly turned and faced her sister-in-law. "What?" There was tremendous pain and bitterness in her eyes. The oxygen cannula and all of the wires and IV lines only made her appearance more haunting. "Look at this, Candace. You can't even visit me. You have to wear that stupid suit and God awful mask. You expect me to enjoy the fact that I am nothing more than a freak show now?"

"No, Carol. I didn't mean that. I can only imagine how that makes you feel. We all hate it. We hate seeing you like this and we hate dressing up in this crap, but I can know it's worse for you. I'm sorry." Candace lowered her face, softly looking directly into Carol's brown eyes.

"Are you? I don't think anyone is sorry anymore." Carol countered angrily.

"I am, Carol. I really am. I want nothing more than for you to have a normal life again." Candace paused and watched Carol for a moment. Carol was very pale and gaunt. This was not the same woman she had grown up with over the past twelve years. This was just a hollow shell that barely resembled Carol. "Carol, why did you do this?"

Carol sighed. The answer was on her tongue just waiting to be spoken, yet Carol could not bring herself to say those words. The two women just looked at each other.

"I... I... I couldn't take it any more, Candace." Carol finally broke the silence. "Life without Alex is empty and disgusting. People have such hatred for me because I'm gay, because your sister was black, and because I have AIDS. I'm not a bad person, Candace." Carol began crying again. "I'm not." Recalling of those thoughts and memories stung tremendously. The pain was far greater than any of her injuries.

Candace carefully rose out of the chair and walked over to Carol. Gently, she rubbed Carol's arm. "I know you're not, sweetie."

Carol looked down at Candace's hand. She, just like all the other visitors, was wearing gloves. Seeing her latex gloved hand made Carol cry even harder.

"I'm sorry, Carol. I really am. I know you're not a bad

person. Anyone who knows you knows that you're not a bad person. We all love you so very much," Candace gently whispered.

"Hey." A warm, soft, familiar voice spoke gently as a shadow entered Carol's room.

"Hi," Carol said warily. She struggled to turn and face the person. Slowly, they walked closer to her bed until the moonlight from the window revealed Alex's face.

"Alex?"

"Hey baby," Alex gently replied.

"What are you doing here? How are you here?"

"I had to be with my woman."

"But, Alex you're..."

"I am not wearing some dumbass bunny suit. We're both sick. I don't care. I want to be here with you, Carol." Alex began carefully removing Carol's various lines, wires and tubing. Carol's neck brace came off and Carol felt no pain. Her IV lines came out without hesitation. The EKG monitor fell silent. Carol's nasal cannula was removed and yet she did not feel her body strain for oxygen.

"Come here," Alex whispered.

Carol slowly rose from the hospital bed and clutched Alex tightly. "I thought you were gone, babe."

"Huh?"

"I thought you died."

"No, Carol. You must be confused from the accident. I've always been with you."

"Thank God. Please don't ever leave me, Alex."

"I won't. I haven't visited because no one would let me. I snuck up here. I am sick of being kept away from the woman I love."

Carol gripped Alex tightly. She didn't ever want to let her go again. Alex's hands were warm and gentle as they wrapped themselves around Carol's tiny waist.

"Let me look at you." Lovingly, Alex pulled Carol back just enough so she could look deeply into her warm, brown eyes. "God, I've missed you" Alex softly kissed Carol.

Carol felt so deprived from Alex's touch and kisses that she let herself just hang on Alex's lips. They continued to share a warm, gentle kiss. As they continued, their passion reemerged and Carol hungered for Alex in every way possible. Carol reached up and held Alex's beautiful face in her delicate hands. Her skin was still as warm and soft as ever.

Alex gently pulled Carol in closer. Alex's hands moved softly over Carol's body and gown. Her tender touch sent shivers up Carol's spine. Still kissing her lover, Carol reached behind her and let her hospital gown float to the floor.

Alex gently slid her hands down Carol's neck and she caressed Carol's breasts. Carol tingled with excitement. She hadn't felt this alive or this in love for ages. Alex's caress sent Carol's soul soaring. Alex gently pulled away. Smiling, she placed her hands under Carol's legs, picked her up and gently laid her on the bed.

Alex smiled brightly down at her partner. Carol was elated to look into Alex's eyes again. Alex's hands carefully wandered over Carol's body. Carol shuddered with excitement. Alex gently kissed and suckled Carol's neck. Carol arched her neck and back in pure ecstasy. Gently, Alex's hands made their way to Carol's legs. Alex teased her by gently running her fingers along the inside of her thighs.

Finally, Alex's hand began gently caressing Carol. Carol softly moaned. Alex covered Carol's small body in warm and passionate kisses as she continued to touch her. Carol's pleasure rose and rose until she exploded in pure ecstasy.

After a few sweet, quiet, tender moments, Alex leaned forward and lovingly kissed Carol on the forehead. "I love you,

Carol." She whispered.

"I love you, Alex."

"Good night, my love," Alex whispered. Carol pulled Alex in and held onto her tightly as she drifted into the sweetest sleep she could remember.

It seemed like only a few minutes had passed when Carol awoke. It was still dark out. Alex wasn't in the bed with her.

"Alex?" Carol asked quietly.

There was no response.

"Alex?" Carol spoke up a bit louder.

Only silence filled the room. Carol looked down and saw that all of her IV lines and EKG leads were still intact. She touched her face and felt that the nasal cannula was still in place. Had Alex put all of the equipment back? Carol looked around desperately. Nothing had been moved in the room. Carol's hospital gown was still tied on. Her casts remained solid over her legs. Fearing that it was all just a dream, Carol shouted. "Alex?"

Carol's cry was so loud that a nurse came rushing in with Byron close behind her.

"Sssshhhh," the nurse said as she carefully injected a clear medication into Carol's IV line.

"What is that?" Byron quietly asked the nurse.

"It's just morphine. It will help with the pain and should help her to fall back asleep."

"Okay, thank you." He sounded worried.

The nurse left.

"Where's Alex?" Carol asked Byron anxiously. Byron could see the fear in her eyes.

"Alex isn't here, Carol."

"But she was."

Byron hesitated before he spoke. “Uhhh... no, Carol. Alex was never here.”

“Byron, she was here with me just a little while ago.” Carol’s speech was already slurred from the morphine.

“Maybe she visited you in a dream, Carol. A wonderful dream.” He paused. “Alex is gone. She’s been dead for a while now. Remember?”

“No!” Carol cried.

Byron gently placed his hand on Carol’s face and stayed with her while she cried herself to sleep. She was once again resting peacefully.

Chapter 6

Dear Alex, I saw you last night. You came to my room. We made love. It was incredible seeing and touching you again. There's something I need to know, though: was it really you or was it just a cruel joke God was playing on me?

Carol's writing was interrupted when Dr. Parker walked into her room, completely done up in his protective suit as usual. Carol slammed her journal shut and hid it under her pillow.

"Do you have any idea what it's like to be on borrowed time?" Carol asked.

"No. What do you mean?" Candace's voice was soft and sincere.

"Since the day I was born, I've been living on borrowed time, Candace. I've been living to die. All my life, I was just waiting. Death has always been right around the corner for me."

"That's not true, Carol."

"Yes it is." Carol replied firmly. "I wasn't even supposed to survive as a child. But I got that transfusion and I did. I was never fully out of the woods, though. And just when I thought I could put all that medical bullshit behind me, I get AIDS. Don't you see? I was never meant to be alive."

"Yes you were. You were meant to be alive, to do something. You always had a purpose, Carol. If you hadn't come along, Alex might not have lived such a wonderful life. She'd probably still be in that apartment alone. She might have even lost her sobriety."

"I doubt that," Carol snapped as she rolled her head to look out the window.

"I don't. You don't realize how happy you made my sister. You gave her so much, Carol. So much more than you could ever know. Trust me."

"I gave her AIDS. That's what I gave her, Candace. The one and only person who could truly accept me as I am and I killed her. She wouldn't have been in the bank if it weren't for me and she certainly wouldn't have gotten AIDS if it weren't for me."

Candace sighed heavily. She had no answer to Carol's harsh self-criticisms. No matter what Candace said or did, Carol was set on self-loathing.

"I should have died as a child. Everyone would have been better off. My father might even still be alive for all I know."

"Carol, stop it! None of that is true. We're *all* glad that you're here. We're all happy that you are a part of our family. We all love you."

"Yeah, right. I'm sure you all feel just like me: just waiting for me to die."

Candace said nothing. It was clear that her words were meaningless to Carol. Carol was living in pure bitterness and self-pity. She obviously didn't care how they felt. Carol was blinded by her own pain and anger. Candace had no way of convincing Carol of the sincerity of her words.

They sat in silence. Candace watched as Carol's mind wandered as she stared at the endlessly grey winter sky outside. She imagined how cold it must have been outside. Candace knew that Carol's heart felt even colder than that.

"So, how have your visits with your friends and family

been, Carol?" Dr. Parker asked. Carol despised his regular visits, but she had no way to escape him.

"Alright, I suppose." Her answer was curt.

"You suppose?" Dr. Parker paused. "Carol, what's been going on? What have you been talking about with everyone?"

"Stuff." She stopped quickly and took a deep breath. "Just stuff."

"Stuff. Wow. Sounds deep, Carol. Somehow I have a feeling that with your current physical and emotional state, you've been talking about more than just 'stuff.'"

"I don't know." Carol carefully positioned herself so she was looking back at him and his protective wear. She drew in a few more deep breaths. "I just shouldn't be here!" Carol finally blurted out.

"Where should you be?" Dr. Parker's face was void of any emotions.

"Dead. I don't know. Just not here. I shouldn't be alive." Carol sighed. "I told Candace how I've always been living on borrowed time. She just didn't get it."

"What didn't she get, Carol?"

"She doesn't understand what it's like to be living just waiting to die. No matter how old you are, you know your death is imminent. All I can do is just wake up every morning and wonder if today is the day I am going to die."

"Today could be the day that *anyone* dies, Carol. What makes it special for you?"

"Regular people don't live like that. They don't sit there and contemplate their own death all the time. They don't know if they're going to get hit by a bus or get cancer. They don't know how they're going to die. I do. I have always known." She looked at Dr. Parker for just a moment and then looked away. "Regular people just don't think the way I do."

"That very well could be true. Does it really matter,

though? So what if you do think differently?"

"It's not about thinking differently. It's about just waiting to die. I, I just never should have been born. Or I at least should have died as an infant because of my anemia. Something. I just shouldn't be here now."

Dr. Parker sat silently and scribbled on his note pad. Carol could only imagine what he was thinking. She sighed in disgust as he continued to write.

Chapter 7

Carol kept pressing the up arrow on the remote. Though the same channels kept showing the same uninteresting shows, she hoped to find something that would sweep her away, if only for a moment, to a place other than her hospital room.

The images on the screen became blurs and the sound was nothing but a mere hum in the background as Carol let her mind wander off.

She wondered about her father.

She wondered what he would have done if he had still been alive when she learned she had AIDS.

She wondered if he'd still be married to her mother.

She wondered if he'd visit her in the hospital.

She wondered how he would have been with Alex.

She wondered what he felt when he was hit by the SUV. She wondered if he felt the impact when he hit the ground. She wondered if he was conscious when the paramedics found him. She wondered if he was cognizant of everything going on while he was rushed into the hospital.

She wondered what his last moments were like.

She wondered what happened to him after he died. Was there nothing waiting for him? Was there a God waiting for him? Did he go to Heaven or Hell? Was he reincarnated? What happened to Walter? What happened to the man that he was? Do people really have souls or is death nearly an endless sleep?

Carol shuddered to think that her father had simply

dissipated into nothing. Yet, she couldn't believe there was anything beyond this life. All she had known was hardship and pain. How could there be anything beyond this terrible existence? She didn't know. All she knew for certain was that whatever waited for her father was waiting for her as well.

Shelby came in all geared up as usual. She was the only person who could wear an incredible amount of hospital garb and still look beautiful. "Good morning, Miss Carol."

"Hey Shelby," Carol replied tiredly. She was sick of this new life in the hospital.

"It's time for us to check your values again."

Carol sighed heavily. Though she wouldn't have to endure the pain of continuous jabs from the needles, she was still aggravated by the feeling that she was nothing more than a guinea pig to the people in this hospital. "Fine," she mumbled.

Shelby obtained her blood samples from one of Carol's many IV ports in sheer silence. Once she had collected all the samples, she stood back up. "Thanks, hon. I'll be back in a little bit with breakfast. Alright?"

"Sure," Carol bitterly responded.

Carol shivered. Despite her blankets and casts, she felt a chill that pierced right through to her bones. Warmth and comfort eluded her. The outside world was still grey and dismal. "It's no wonder people call Missouri 'misery,'" Carol said to herself.

"How has everything been, Carol?" Dr. Parker asked. Carol despised his presence more with each visit.

"The same. I'm stuck in this bed with these tubes, that window and that TV. Nothing has changed."

"Carol, you seem very angry. Your family says that you weren't an angry person before. What's going on?"

Carol glared at Dr. Parker. How pretentious of him. He had no right to speak to anyone in the family and he certainly had no right to ask her questions like that. She stared at him for several minutes. Finally she turned her head away and stared out the window. "Is this where I'm supposed to have some kind of emotional breakdown while I'm looking out the window and we have a special moment while music gently plays in the background?" Carol's cynicism was shocking even to Dr. Parker.

"Well... if that's what you want."

"No. What I want is to be left alone."

Carol heard Dr. Parker sigh. "Alright, Carol. I'm not going to push you any more. I will still visit, but you tell me what you want to, when you want to. Deal?"

"Yeah," Carol mumbled.

Dr. Parker rose and walked out of her room. Carol couldn't even smile, though she was relieved he was gone. She laid there in silence and let her mind wander. Carol continued to silently watch the outside world long after he had left.

Byron and Candace slowly walked out of Carol's room. She finally fell asleep. Yet another day had passed in her mediocre existence in this hospital. Just as they began to walk towards the elevator, Will ran after them.

"Byron!" He called out.

Byron and Candace turned around.

"Hi," Will said puffing as he tried to catch his breath. "Is Carol still up?"

"No, Will. Why? Can't it wait?"

Bill took a few deep breaths. "Robyn... Robyn and I just

came from the vet. We had to put Sugar to sleep. She was so old... and she had cancer. I hated to do it without talking to Carol, but..."

"Say no more, Will." Byron grimaced. "We understand."

"Are you coming back tomorrow? Will you be able to tell her?" Will asked anxiously.

"I don't think that's a good idea, Will." Byron said gently.

"Why not?"

"Will, she lost our sister. She totaled Alex's car. She's already lost so much in her life. If she hears that Sugar is gone too, I'm afraid that it might send her into a terrible depression," Byron answered. "God only knows what she would do. Sugar was the last normal thing she had. Sugar was all she had left of her old life. I'm afraid she'll think that losing Sugar means she has nothing to live for – nothing to go home to."

Will paused. "I never thought of that."

"It's fine," Candace said. "You didn't want to hurt her. You wanted to be honest with her. Normally we'd both tell you to be completely honest. Carol's in a bad place, Will. We're both really worried about her. I just don't want to risk making things worse than they already are."

"Yeah, I get it."

"And when you are able to visit, just don't bring it up. If she asks, just say everything is fine." Byron added.

Will thought about their words for a few seconds. "Okay. That sounds like it's the best thing to do. Thanks."

With that, the elevator came up to their floor and the doors opened. "Mind if I join you?" Will asked.

Candace waddled through the doors first. Byron let Will go in next and then he walked into the elevator. They all went downstairs to return to their lives.

"Hey Candace," Carol said without turning her head. She saw Candace's geared up reflection in the window.

"Hey," Candace huffed as she awkwardly sat her pregnant body on the chair. "How are you?"

"I don't know. The same, I guess."

"Carol, what can we do to get you out of this?"

"Out of what? This hospital?"

"This funk," Candace snapped back.

"Let me die." Carol mumbled.

"Carol, you have got to stop talking like that."

Carol slowly rolled over to look at Candace. The young woman had never sounded so harsh to Carol. She took several deep breaths before she spoke. "You wouldn't understand, C."

"Try me." Candace said in a sharp tone.

Carol sighed. "Candace, my whole life has been nothing but a giant fuck up."

"You can't say that," Candace interrupted her.

"Yes, I can. I can say it quite easily. It's only the truth."

"Candace, my mother couldn't have any more kids because of me. My parents lost and sacrificed so much because of me. My father died because I came out to my parents that night. My best friend killed himself because he got AIDS from me. My college roommate OD'd because of me. Alex died because I gave her AIDS and we went to the bank that day because of me. You'd still have your sister's car if I would have just killed myself right. Don't you see? I can't do anything right. I have fucked up *everything* in my life!"

Candace took a deep breath. "Okay, let's go through this one by one." She was speaking as if Carol was one of her patients. "Your mother couldn't have kids because of a condition that she had, not because of you."

"It *was* me. She always said it was my fault."

"What if that's not true, Carol? What if she was wrong?"

Carol lay silently in her bed. She had never entertained the notion that her mother could have been wrong about that. Carol was at a loss for words.

"Your mother had placenta previa, not you." Candace continued. "You didn't give her that. It's just a condition. A condition that *she* had. She blamed you because she wasn't able to accept reality. Got it?"

"Yes, your parents did have to sacrifice a lot because of your illness. But that's what parents do, Carol. Once you become a parent, it's all about your child. It's no longer about you. I'm sure the sacrifices were hard, but that was the right thing – the only thing to do. You didn't choose to be sick. You were born that way. Your parents did what they had to do. You do not get to blame yourself for that."

Carol sighed. She was having difficulty accepting all the things Candace was saying.

"Your father did not die because of you. Were you the one driving the SUV that hit him?"

Carol didn't respond.

"Did you drive that SUV that night?" Candace was loud and unyielding.

"No," Carol muttered.

"Exactly. The only person responsible for your father's death was the person driving that SUV, not you. Do you understand?"

"Yeah," Carol whispered.

"As for Ed, well, you don't know why Ed killed himself, Carol. You cannot take the blame. He didn't even tell his parents. It could have been anything."

"But..." Carol started to speak.

"But what? Is it possible? Sure. But you don't know, Carol. You'll never know for sure. You are going to have to make peace with not knowing the truth. You need to accept that you will never know whether or not you gave him AIDS."

"I never meant to hurt anyone... not even Ed." Carol said under her breath.

Candace paused and took a deep breath. "Girl, you amaze me sometimes."

"Why is that?" Carol asked. She was feeling so confused.

"You still call Ed your best friend."

"Well yeah. He was." Carol answered without hesitation.

"Carol... ummmm... how do I say this? Carol, how do you remain friends with someone who tried to do that to you?"

Carol looked up at Candace. She was confused for just a moment before she fully understood. "Oh." Carol paused briefly. "I don't know, C. We always had such a great friendship and his family was so good to me. We had been friends for ages. I mean, yes, something happened, but we *all* fuck up. We all make mistakes. You can't kill a friendship because of *one* mistake."

"One mistake? Are you serious? A mistake is one thing, but... but that was something completely different." Candace's eyes were filled with sympathy and sadness.

"Honestly," Carol started. "I think he thought sex would be a way to comfort me and things just got messed up. I really don't think his intentions were bad. Ed wasn't like that. You have to believe me. Please don't assume anything about him based on that one night. You can't judge a person based on one incident. I've always hated being judged by others, so I'm definitely not going to judge anyone else."

Candace remained silent for a moment. "Did he ever apologize? How did you put it behind you?"

Carol looked away. "Yeah, he apologized. Sort of. In his

own 'Ed' kind of way. And I just didn't think about it. Not addressing it makes sure it doesn't hurt you. Just like college. Studying and working my ass off made sure I couldn't feel the pain of my dad's death. It's just how I deal, I guess. Better than feeling all the pain and guilt."

Candace sighed. "Guilt? Damn it! Here we go again. You want to take the blame for every tragedy that ever occurred in this world? What about Vietnam? Was that your fault? Was the Holocaust your fault? Was nine-eleven your fault? If you're going to take the blame for everyone's deaths, you might as well take the blame for those... and the crusades, too while you're at it."

Candace was getting loud. Surprisingly loud. Carol watched the sweat trickle down Candace's face and neck.

"Oh, and don't let me forget your old college roommate. Same goes for her."

"But, Marlene died after she saw *me*." Carol tried to justify her guilt.

"Oh please. You don't know what happened with her. She was a junkie, Carol. It could have been a simple over-dose having absolutely nothing to do with you," Candace said sternly.

Carol had never seen Candace so intense. For the first time since she had met Candace, Carol was in awe of her.

"Look Carol, I will give you that Alex got AIDS from you. Yes. She got it from you. But you know what else she got from you? She got twelve years of love and devotion like she had never seen before. She learned how to drive a stick from you. She got a great surprise birthday from you. She got a house and a dog from you, a family of her own. Do you have any idea how tremendous that is? Very few people get a loving and devoted family and a home to call their own especially at such a young age like you two. You gave her so much.

"She got great memories from you. Do you know how

many times she told me about the things you did for her on her birthdays or your anniversaries? I heard about you two singing to Hendrix more times than I care to count. She always talked about how you would sit through *The Princess Bride* for her. If you want me to keep going, I can. She and I had a million conversations about all the great things you did for her, so you had better stop talking about bullshit that isn't true!" Candace was now yelling.

Carol's fear and confusion could be seen beneath her various wires and tubes. Realizing her tone, Candace quieted down. "Carol, you loved my sister. You've loved all of us. You taught us how to truly accept people regardless of color or orientation. You came with us to visit our mother every year until she died. You put up with my punk ass for all these years. You stayed with us while Byron was ripping you apart because of AIDS. Damn it, Carol. You're not a fuck up." Candace turned away to hide her tears. "Did you ever stop to think about how your words might be affecting *us*?"

Carol was silent for a moment. Never before had she seen her sister-in-law so passionate, or so hurt. "No," she softly replied.

"Carol, you aren't the only one hurting here. I can promise you that. You've taken this way too far."

"Candace," Carol said as she tried to sit herself up. "I'm sorry. I didn't mean to hurt you. It's just, well, I always heard how I ruined my parents' lives and everything. My whole life I have been nothing but a fuck up. My own mother told me that. I guess I just got used to thinking that way about everything."

"Your mother was wrong, Carol." Candace's tone was firm but loving. "I promise you that she could not have been further from the truth. It's not your fault. Shit happens. That's life."

"Look at *our* family, Carol. My mother was a prostitute. My sister was an alcoholic until a couple of years before she met you. Byron has his own weird prejudices. We aren't perfect, are we?"

"No," Carol quietly replied.

"Nobody's life is perfect. That's just the way life is. It doesn't mean it's your fault or anyone else's fault. It's just life." Candace paused to take some deep breaths. "Can I be completely honest, Carol?"

"Yes," Carol replied hesitantly.

"Carol, you are an extremely sensitive person. I think it's great. You've always been sympathetic and caring towards other people. You show a gentleness to people that is beyond rare in this day and age. You are so compassionate. It's a fantastic trait. But it has also made you too sensitive. Way too sensitive. You take *everything* personally. Every little thing that was said or happened in your life, you took it on as your own. You take everything personally and to the nth degree at that! You have to learn to have that same compassion, but not be so overly sensitive. Does that make sense?"

Carol paused before she spoke. "Sort of."

"Carol, you're an incredible person. We all love you and we always will. You just need to realize that not everything bad that happens is because of you, okay?"

"Okay," Carol sighed.

Slowly, Candace pushed herself up out of the chair. "Sweetie, I need to go home. I have got to rest. The baby's moving around like there's no tomorrow. I hate to leave, but I'm really glad we had this talk."

"Yeah, me too." Carol said. She looked up at Candace. "I love you," she said tenderly.

"I love you too, Carol."

They smiled at each other and then Candace slowly made her way out of Carol's room. Carol carefully rolled back onto her side so she could look out the window and contemplate everything Candace had just said.

Chapter 8

"Good morning, Miss Carol." Shelby said brightly as she entered Carol's room with her breakfast. "How are you today?"

"Fine, thanks." Carol dismissed the question. "Hey Shelby. Why do you do this?"

"Do what?"

"Work here every day. Put up with assholes like me."

Shelby chuckled. "You are anything but an asshole, Ms. Mathers. You're a pleasure to see every day."

"I do this because I want to help people. I know that sounds corny, but it's true. I like to hope that I can help brighten someone's day. There's nothing better than seeing a patient go home and to hear them thank us. To be a part of that person's recovery is an incredible experience."

Carol paused to think. "I suppose it is. But what about when your patient dies?"

"That's tough," Shelby said in a quiet tone. "We hate to lose them, but it's a part of life around here. We just hope that we made their time here as comfortable as possible. Sometimes death is the best thing because of the pain that they're in. It's not all bad."

Carol looked up at her for a few silent moments. "Shelby, let's be honest. You and I both know I'm not ever leaving here."

"You never know. I've seen people in much worse condition walk out of here. Anything is possible."

Carol inhaled a deep breath. She prayed Shelby was wrong. The world outside of her hospital room was a gloomy and scary place. “Will you miss me when I’m gone?” Carol asked quietly.

“What did you say?” Shelby asked. She hadn’t heard Carol’s question.

“Will you remember me after I’m gone?”

Shelby slouched a little. She hated it when patients would ask her questions like this. “Carol, as much as I have an impact on my patients, they all have an impact on me. You will not be forgotten. I promise. Okay?”

“Yeah.” Carol whispered as she diverted her attention to the grey world outside her window. She hoped Shelby wasn’t lying, but Carol felt so cynical and calloused it was nearly impossible to know who was genuine and who wasn’t.

“Carol, I mean it. I won’t forget you. Ever.” Shelby gently placed her hand on Carol’s shoulder. Carol slowly rolled over and their eyes met. Shelby smiled luminously under her mask.

“Thanks,” Carol replied weakly.

Dear Alex, I’m not even sure what to say today. My life hasn’t changed since I last wrote to you. They still suck out my blood, pump me full of all kinds of drugs, tell me gibberish. Your family visits every day. Candace is extremely pregnant. I don’t think she can carry this baby much longer. She is literally about to pop. She’s still with Tyrone. They seem to be doing really well.

I haven’t seen too much of Erin. Byron’s here quite a bit. We talk, but it’s just weird. It’s always strained conversation. I think he wishes that I died more than I do. I haven’t seen Will and Robyn or Dave and John in a while. I miss them.

I miss you more, though. I wish that life could get back to the way it was, to the way it used to be with you. All I want is what we had, our life, back, but I know that will never happen.

Candace and I had a long talk the other day. She said I was too sensitive. Do you think so? I mean, she made some great points and all. Maybe she's right. She said I needed to stop blaming myself for everything. Do you think that too? But where does someone draw the line between responsibility and apathy? Everyone needs to be held accountable for their words and actions. We all know that. So, I'm responsible for my own actions, right? If that's the case and my actions result in someone's death, like my Dads, Ed's, YOURS, then I am to blame. Right? I don't know. I don't know anything. I'm just all confused.

What I do know is that I hate this place and I hate my life without you. I really hope this is over soon so I can be with you again. There's nothing for me here, that's for sure. I guess I'll just leave it at that for now. I love you honey.

Carol slowly closed the book and hid it under her pillow. The clock on her wall read just after three in the morning. She pressed the call button for the nurse so she could get some more morphine, and hopefully some sleep.

"Nothing is permanent, Doc. Not a job, not a home, not a family. Hell, not even tattoos are permanent because the people who wear them eventually die." Carol rambled. She was watching the outside world through her window just the way she always did. It was a far more preferable scene than looking at Dr. Parker.

"That's very true, Carol. Everything in life *is* fleeting." Dr. Parker paused for a moment. "What made you think about that?" He asked through his mask.

Carol sighed. "I don't know. Everything. I was just thinking about it. Everyone and everything in my life has always gone away. Nothing ever stayed the same. Nothing ever lasted."

Dr. Parker waited before he spoke up. "You know, I don't know if I'd say that, Carol. You've actually had several parts of your life that have lasted. Haven't you been with Dawson since college? I know you'd still be with Alex. You've been in your home for a number of years now. So there have been things that have been long-lasting. Some things have, in fact, been permanent. Yes, your life has changed, but you've also had quite a bit of stability. Stability that many people never experience."

"If you say so," Carol mumbled.

They sat in silence for a few moments.

"What do you want, Carol? What would you like to last? Aside from Alex, what would you like to be permanent?"

Carol slowly turned her head and looked at him. "Permanent sunsets," she quietly answered.

"Permanent sunsets? What does that mean? Why do you want permanent sunsets?"

"Who doesn't love a beautiful sunset?" Carol replied. "It's the end of the day. The sky doesn't even look real. It looks like a painting. You're calm and peaceful. The world just stops spinning for you to enjoy that moment, that sunset. Everything looks so perfect. Life is perfect in that moment. I want to see that, to feel that. Not just for a moment, but all the time. It just seems so wonderful." Carol paused and thought about the serenity she'd enjoy from permanent sunsets. "Yeah, that's what I want, Dr. Parker. Permanent sunsets," she said decisively.

Dr. Parker simply nodded in agreement with a slight smile.

Dave and John stood on either side of Carol's bed.

"How are you, Carol?" John asked.

"As good as one can be, I guess."

"We miss you," Dave said.

"I miss you guys too," Carol replied. "How have you two been?"

"About the same," John answered her. "Dave is still working with Ludlow and Kepwick, thank God. I got laid off because of the economy. I'm actually waiting for a call back from the grocery store for a job. It's not glamorous, but it's an income. I'll take that over the lack of an income I've had for the past several months."

"I am so sorry, John. You deserve so much better than that." Carol said.

"Thanks. It's okay, really. It's just the way things are right now." John responded.

"I guess I'm lucky that Dawson is still around." Carol replied.

"Yeah, you are." Dave said. "It's bad out there. I'm lucky I was able to stay with Lisa. Everyone is cutting back tremendously."

"Wow," Carol said quietly. She knew that the economy had plummeted, but since Alex died Carol hadn't been paying attention to the news. She had no idea just how severe the situation really was. It was frightening to see people she knew be so deeply affected by the economic crash.

"Yeah. We..." John was cut off when Byron entered the room.

"Hi guys," Byron said.

"Hey Byron." John and Dave replied in unison.

Everyone stood in awkward silence for a moment.

"Would you guys mind if I had a few words with Carol alone?" Byron asked.

"No, not at all." John replied. He walked around and grabbed Dave's hand. "Come on, honey."

"Bye, Carol. We'll catch you later."

"Okay. Bye, boys. Please come back soon."

"We will." John said.

"Bye." Byron said quickly.

"Bye," both Dave and John said as they walked out.

"What's up, Byron?" Carol asked with a hint of suspicion in her voice.

"Something I should have done a long time ago."

Byron took a deep breath and looked intently into Carol's eyes. "Carol, I'm sorry," he said. "I'm sorry I gave you flack about being a white girl the first time I met you. I'm sorry for all the hurtful things I said to you when you told us you and Alex had AIDS. I'm sorry for how poorly I treated you after Alex died. I'm just so sorry for all of it." Byron broke down and began crying. "All of my life, I always had to watch out for Alex. She was my twin, but we were so different. I had to protect her. I thought I was protecting her when you came around. I couldn't see that you were protecting her far better than I ever could. I see that now, though. I am so sorry." Byron sobbed.

Carol was silent while Byron cried. She was unsure how to react.

"I'm sorry," Byron sobbed again.

"It's okay, B. You don't need to apologize," she said softly.

"Yes I do," he sniffled. "I'm sorry."

"It's okay. I still love you, Byron." Carol answered with a smile.

Byron looked up at her. His eyes grew bright through the tears. "I love you too, Carol."

Sweetly smiling at each other, they shared a silent moment. They didn't need to say anything. They understood each other.

"You should go home to your wife, B. I'm sure she misses you." Carol spoke softly, but wisely.

"I don't want to leave you alone." He wiped away a tear.

"It's okay. I'm not alone. I have enough nurses and doctors coming in here to keep me occupied all night. Okay?" This was the first time Byron had seen Carol smile in ages.

Byron placed his hands over his face. "Okay," he said as he wiped away the remaining tears. "If you insist. I'll see you later, though." Byron smiled at her.

"Okay," Carol beamed back.

Byron took a deep breath and rubbed his eyes. After a moment, he regained his composure. Byron left Carol's room quietly.

"Will! I haven't seen you ages. How are you? How's Nate?" Carol was so excited to see her dear friend.

"He's good, Carol. You were right about him. He's been a perfect asset to the company." Will turned to look behind him. "He was with me, but I must have lost him somewhere." He turned back to Carol, "How are you sweetie?"

"Okay. Well, as okay as I can be all things considered."

"Yeah," Will softly replied. "Robyn and I miss you."

"I miss you guys too. I wish you'd visit more."

"Me too. Time is just so limited. Working, trying to run the company in your absence. I don't know how you did it, Carol. It's killing me. I am clearly not as talented as you."

"Yes you are. You just got thrown into the fire. At least I had Greg teaching me before he left. I'm sure you're doing fine."

Nate finally walked in. His appearance was comical as the bunny suit he wore was far too big for his petite frame.

"Hey Nate. How are you?" Carol's eyes were bright and cheerful despite her environment.

"I'm good," he answered quietly. "How are you? We all miss you at work and at group."

"I'm doing fine, Nate." Carol's smile and demeanor were genuine. It was the first time in a long time that she could say she was genuinely happy. "I hear you're doing well at Dawson."

"I'm doing the best I can, Carol."

"I'm sure it's great. I always had faith in you."

"Thanks," he said meekly.

"You said group misses me too?" Carol was surprised that the people from group would notice that she had been gone, let alone miss her.

"Oh yeah. Everyone asks about you."

"Wow. That's really sweet," she said in pleasant surprise.

"You've had a tremendous impact on a lot of us, Carol. Group just isn't the same without you."

Carol was taken aback by Nathan's comment. She never thought that group liked her or that she would have affected anyone there. After a few moments of taking it all in, she said, "tell everyone I send my love."

"I will," Nate replied.

"And you tell Robyn that I send my love to her too," Carol said as she turned to Will.

"Will do, boss," Will smiled.

"How's sugar? I've been meaning to ask you."

Will was floored. What was he supposed to tell her? He remembered what Byron and Candace had said. "She's good, Carol. She's really happy and doing just fine. Robyn loves her, you know that." Will hoped he had covered the truth well enough.

"Good," Carol closed her eyes and smiled. "It's so great having you both here. I've miss you guys! I just wish..."

Carol was cut off by a strange nurse coming into her room. "Alright, Miss Mathers, it's time for your evening medications."

"Where's Shelby?" Carol was confused. She didn't recognize this nurse and Shelby always gave her the evening medications before she left for the day.

"She's with another patient." This nurse seemed cold and distant.

"Oh," Carol said sadly.

"You gentlemen are going to have to leave now." The nurse looked at Will and Nate sternly.

"But they just got here," Carol protested.

"I'm sorry. Hospital regulations."

Carol cursed under her breath. "Sorry, guys. Please come back soon, okay?"

"We will," Will said.

"Yeah," Nate agreed.

The three took a moment to just smile at each other. Carol's brown eyes spoke of her disappointment and loneliness. Will and Nate hesitated. They hated to see her so upset.

The nurse glared at the two men. They glanced back at her. Their gazes went back to Carol. They mouthed the words, "I'm sorry." Slowly, they exited Carol's room.

Chapter 9

Dave and John entered Carol's room and found a crowd around Carol's bed. Byron and Erin, Tyrone and Candace and Will and Robyn all stood around their unconscious friend.

"Oh God, it's bad?" Dave said.

"It's not good," Tyrone said turning to Dave.

"What's going on?" John calmly asked.

"Her liver and kidneys don't look good. They were about to perform their first surgery when the blood work showed that her kidneys couldn't handle the anesthetics." Byron said, trying to remain stoic. His voice still faltered as he spoke, though.

"How come they didn't catch this before?" John asked. His tone indicated his dismay.

"They knew her levels were a little high, but when the surgeon took a look he said he didn't want to take the risk. So, he backed out." Tyrone answered.

"How bad is it? I mean, is she going to make it?" Dave asked.

"Yeah," Will sighed. "It's not great news, but the kidneys aren't failing."

"Yet." Byron said firmly.

Will shot Byron a nasty look. "Let's not make any pronouncements yet. They're simply postponing her surgery until her organ function is better. You heard the doctor, Byron. The levels are elevated, but not in failure."

Carol mumbled something softly. Candace looked over at

her, but Carol still seemed to be resting quietly. Candace turned back to the group as they continued to discuss Carol's condition.

"Dad," Carol mumbled. This time, she was audible. Her eyes rolled around for a moment before closing again.

The group all fell silent and watched her.

"Dad," she moaned again. "I want my dad," she called out in a child-like manner.

Chills ran up everyone's spine.

"Dad? Don't people normally say they want their mommy?" Dave whispered.

"Yeah, but she doesn't have a relationship with her mom. She was always close to her dad. He was the one that was always there for her, but he passed away before she went to college." Candace gently stated.

"Oh God," John whispered. "That's terrible. We had no idea..."

"Dad!" Carol's cry was weak, but still disturbing to the crowd around her.

Byron sighed, trying to shake the eerie feeling he had because of Carol's cries. They all continued to watch Carol in her uneasy sleep. Not wanting to stay, but not wanting to leave her, they stood silently, just watching and concerned. They wanted Carol to have some peace.

Shelby walked into Carol's room. Just as she did, the sunlight came through Carol's window much brighter.

"Wow, you brought the sun with you!" Carol smiled.

"Just for you," Shelby flirtatiously answered. "How are you this morning?"

"Just another day in paradise," Carol sighed as she

replied.

“Well, paradise is going to be changed a bit today.” Shelby walked over and stood next to Carol’s bed. She gently placed her hand on Carol’s shoulder. Carol looked up at the smiling blonde beauty. “I am going to give you your bath today.”

“Huh? What?” Carol was perplexed. Shelby never bathed her before, that was always an aid or another nurse. Deirdre was usually the one who helped Carol with such tasks. Why had things changed?

“Don’t worry, just relax.” Shelby’s tone was almost seductive. She helped Carol lean forward, and she began untying Carol’s hospital gown. The gown slowly slid off Carol, exposing her pale, frail body. Shelby took a warm wash cloth and began to gently pat Carol’s neck with it. “How’s that?” She whispered into Carol’s ear. Without waiting for a response, Shelby began to kiss Carol’s ear. She tenderly way made her way down Carol’s neck.

“What, what are you doing? What’s going on?” Carol tried to remain focused despite Shelby’s incredibly enticing kisses.

“Sssshhh. Relax, honey. You know you’ve wanted this from the beginning.” Shelby sat on the edge of Carol’s bed. She let her hands lightly wander all over Carol’s body. She leaned in and tenderly kissed Carol. Her lips were warm and erotic. She was hard to resist. After a few exciting moments, Carol pulled away.

“Wait. No, no. This isn’t right. We can’t be doing this. I’m supposed to be with Alex,” Carol protested.

Shelby ignored Carol’s words and continued her ministrations.

“I said, stop!” Carol exclaimed as she pushed Shelby off of her. “I’m supposed to be with Alex. You need to stop this.” Carol was firm.

"Forget Alex," Shelby whispered. "She's dead anyway," she said coldly as her hand slid higher and higher on Carol's thigh.

Unable to control her body, Carol started to become putty in Shelby's hands. Her eyes closed and her body tingled with excitement. Shelby took Carol's hand and placed it on her chest. "You've always wanted me," Shelby whispered.

With amazing strength and bravado, Carol sat up. "No. No, I don't want you, Shelby. I mean you're beautiful, but I'm supposed to be with Alex. I can't do this."

"Fine!" Shelby jumped back. "Just remember, you see me every day!" She violently wagged a finger at Carol. "You'll regret this!" She yelled. Shelby jumped off the bed, stormed out of the room and slammed the door behind her.

Carol jumped when the door slammed. She looked around the room, her heart still racing.

Shelby walked into Carol's room. Carol looked at herself. Her gown was still on. Her legs and pelvis were still stuck in the casts. Her urinary catheter lay perfectly still. Everything looked undisturbed. Shelby wore a bright, beautiful smile. As she approached Carol's bed, the sunlight streamed through Carol's window much brighter.

"Wow, you brought the sun with you!" Carol said without thinking.

"Just for you," Shelby answered. "How are you this morning?"

"Just another day in paradise," Carol replied. The feeling of déjà vu was making Carol feel uncomfortable. What was going on? Fear and confusion gripped Carol. She looked all around her room. She could feel her heart was still pounding. Carol's puzzled eyes followed Shelby. She didn't seem angry or vindictive at all. Carol tried desperately to calm herself.

"Sorry the accommodations aren't better, Carol." Shelby paused. "It's time for your morning medications."

Carol looked at Shelby puzzled. “Huh?”

“I’m sorry. I must have startled you. You were sleeping a few minutes ago. I didn’t mean to scare you awake. It’s just after seven, hon. it’s time for your morning medications.”

Carol looked at Shelby for a few more moments.

“Are you okay, Carol?” Shelby seemed genuinely concerned.

“Ummmm... yeah. Yeah, I’m okay, Shelby. Just had a weird dream. That’s all.”

“Oh, I’m sorry.” Shelby answered lightly as she slowly injecting medications into Carol’s IV lines.

“Hey, Candace,” Carol spoke into the hospital room phone. It was strange to talk to Candace over the phone rather than in person, but Candace was not feeling well enough to visit.

“Hey Carol,” Candace grunted.

“I want you to know that I’ve been thinking a lot about what you said.”

“What I said about what?”

“You know, being too sensitive and all.”

“Oh yeah.” Candace paused, and Carol could hear her taking a drink. “So?”

“Well, I’m not sure if you’re right.”

“Why couldn’t I be right, Carol? Is it because I’m so much younger than you?”

“No, no. Not at all.” Carol hadn’t even considered that notion. “Age was never a factor, C. I - it’s just that, well, I... uhhh... not only am I a failure, Candace. I’m also a fake.”

“A fake? What do you mean, Carol?”

"Just that I, I don't know. I guess I kind of muddled my way through life. Nothing I ever did was original or... it's just that I've faked a lot of things, like what I know or how to do certain things."

"Carol, I don't understand you at all. What are you trying to say?"

"I, I don't know," Carol began crying. "I just feel like I never really did anything because I was good at it."

"When I studied history, I skated by based on what my dad told me and all of his books. I wasn't a good history student. It wasn't a passion I worked hard at or anything. I had my dad to rely on, sort of. It was easy, I didn't put in any real effort. I faked my way through those classes while the other students studied endlessly."

"Everything that I know about computers was just replicating what Will or Greg Dawson said or did. It was nothing I did on my own. I was a phony even when it came to my knowledge. I just copied other people.

"Running Dawson, too, was simply a matter of copying Greg's work. I couldn't have come up with all of that on my own. I'm not that smart."

"I just counterfeited my way through those things."

Candace sighed heavily on the other end. "Carol, was your love for my sister fake?"

"No! Of course not. I do love her. Always have, always will. I just..."

"You just what?" Candace was abrupt, but sympathetic.

"I just knew that I wasn't good enough. Because I had faked my way through school and all, I had to make sure that I somehow seemed worthy of her."

Candace was silent for a moment. "Carol, is that why you bought my sister the house? Because you felt like you weren't good enough? Because you felt you weren't smart enough or were somehow inferior to her?"

"Yes," Carol sobbed. "I loved her so much but she was so smart and could do so much with her knowledge and experience on her own. She didn't need me. I knew I wasn't good enough for her. I wanted to make up for my shortcomings somehow." Carol wept non-stop.

"Oh honey," Candace stopped. "Carol," she said softly. "That's not true. That's not true at all."

"Okay, so you used what you learned from your father and his books to get you through college. We're supposed to use our family, friends and various resources. That's why they're there. You didn't do anything wrong. And let me tell you something, you are smart. If you weren't smart, you wouldn't have graduated second in your class. You can't fake your way through that."

"I was only second. Not good enough, not good enough to be first," Carol stammered.

"Carol, second is better than most people even dream of. You were, no, you are good enough. You were good enough for college. You were good enough for everything you did."

"You were definitely good enough for Alex. You loved her like no one had ever loved her before. Even B, God knows, he tried. He loved her through the worst of it, but even he couldn't love or accept her the way you did. You gave her a joy that I had never seen in her before. She was so hurt and depressed before you. You came along and she literally lit up, Carol."

"Look, she loved everything you gave her. Who wouldn't? You bought her the best of the best." She continued without missing a beat. "You got her sweet sentimental gifts. "You got her the house she wanted. You cooked for her on special occasions. That meant the world to her because she knew that not only did it come from the heart, but it was something extra. You did something you normally don't do. She appreciated that gesture more than you'll ever know."

"You completely accepted and respected her sobriety. You accepted her twin brother who would have had no problem putting a hit out on you. You put up with her bitter, wise-ass younger sister. You went to see her disfigured and debilitated mother every year. You supported her through Mom's death."

"You and Alex went to that group together. You didn't abandon her in the darkest hour you both shared. You stayed with her night and day at the end, Carol. You never left my sister's side. Not in twelve years. That is incredible." Candace finally paused for a breath. "Don't you get it, Carol? You're a far greater person than you realize."

Carol simply sniffled into the phone.

"Carol, you are not a fake and you certainly are not inferior. Not to Alex. Not to anyone. You got that?"

Carol inhaled a few deep breaths. "Yeah," she feebly replied. "You know, Candace, I couldn't have these conversations with anyone else but you. You remind me a lot of your sister in certain ways. You listen to me. No one else would understand. Alex was like that, too. Thanks."

"Thank you, Carol. That was the nicest thing anyone has ever said about me. It's an honor to be like my sister."

"I love you, Candace." Carol's voice began cracking again.

"I love you too," Candace gently replied.

"When are you coming back?" Carol's sobbing sounded pathetic. She sounded like a lost, scared child.

"Soon, sweetie. I'll be there as soon as I can, okay?"

"I need you," Carol sniffled into the phone.

"I'm never far away." Candace said sweetly, hoping that she could bring Carol some solace. Candace took a deep breath and prayed a silent prayer while Carol sobbed into the phone.

Chapter 10

"How are you, this morning?" Dr. Parker asked.

"Alright, I guess. I just wish they'd do the first surgery already. I'm so sick of all this pain and all these drugs. And the waiting," Carol replied.

"I can understand that, Carol. Unfortunately, with your condition, these things take longer."

"I know," Carol mumbled. She looked out the window. The sun was trying desperately to peek through the thick layer of clouds. Sometimes the sun would manage a quick glimmer, but the cloud cover was thick so its appearances were brief at best. "Doc, what happens when we die?"

"What do you mean, Carol?" Dr. Parker asked.

"What happens when we die? Is there a heaven? Do we just die and nothing happens? Are we reincarnated?"

"What do you believe happens, Carol?"

Carol turned her head and gave Dr. Parker an angry, contemptuous look. "I don't know. That's why I'm asking. I am dying, you know. It might be good if I knew what was coming."

"That's the funny thing about death. We all die, but no one knows what will happen. That's where faith comes in."

"Oh, great. Here it comes," Carol sneered.

"No, no. I'm not going to endorse faith or proselytize anyone, Carol. I'm not a priest or rabbi or any kind of clergy. Everyone believes different things. I have no authority to tell people what is or isn't right to believe. You need to figure that out for yourself." He raised his hands in question. "What do you think happens?"

"I don't know," Carol answered. There was a hint of vulnerability in her voice.

"What would you like to think?" Dr. Parker kindly asked. "What would be comforting to you?"

"I'm not sure. I mean, I hate to think that my dad and Alex just stopped existing completely. But I can't imagine a heaven with cherubs playing harps and all."

Dr. Parker nodded. "You mentioned reincarnation. Do you think that's possible?"

"I guess anything is possible, but it's weird to think that my dad came back as a cat or something."

"Maybe he came back as another person."

"No. I don't want that to be true. He's my dad. He left us too early. It's not right if he's off having fun with some other family."

Dr. Parker nodded his head. "That makes sense. You felt that he left a lot of unfinished business. You've said he was the only real parent in your life."

"Yeah," Carol said in a defeated tone.

"Okay, what else is out there?"

"I don't know," Carol replied harshly.

"Well, Carol. The reality is religions and beliefs run the gamut. You really could believe anything and everything. Maybe you should think about what you believe, what makes sense or feels right to you. You never know. Maybe you'll come up with the answer."

"Thanks," Carol sighed in exasperation.

"Carol, it seems vague, I know. These are the kinds of decisions you need to make on your own. We can certainly discuss them, but only you know what belief is best for you.

Do you understand?"

"Alright," Carol huffed.

Carol could recognize those bright, rich green eyes anywhere. She was surprised that he was here visiting. "Dr. J! What are you doing here?" She was enthusiastic.

"Checking on my patient. How long have you been here?" He asked, his voice muffled behind his mask.

"I'm not sure. Too long"

"Well, at least they finally contacted me."

"What's going on?"

"Nothing. The hospital should have contacted me as soon as you were admitted, that's all. I reviewed your chart. They haven't done anything wrong, I just like to have a say in my patients' care."

"You're the best, Dr. J. It's nice to see a familiar face. I'm sick of seeing new people all the time. It seems like just when I start to get used to a doctor or nurse, someone new comes in and the other one just vanishes.

"Do you know whatever happened to Dr. Ramone?"

"Hospital bureaucracy. They switched you over to someone else, but now I have him as your primary while you're in here. He'll be answering to you and me. You do need that familiarity, especially considering your condition."

"What about the shrink, Dr. Parker?"

"Sorry, Carol. There's nothing I can do about that. You need to have your regular visits with him because of your attempted suicide."

Carol paused. Suicide. No one had ever said that word, at least not out loud. Not in front of her, anyway. Suddenly, her actions took on a whole new meaning and feeling. The word stung Carol, but she knew it was the right word. It was true. She had tried to commit suicide. "Yeah," she agreed quietly. She looked away in shame. She wished she could have been stronger, or had succeeded. Having Dr. J know exactly what happened was humiliating.

"Carol, you need to stay strong," Dr. J said. Carol looked up at him. "I know things have been rough on you. This is not going to be easy to get through. Your body is going to be tested over and over again. I need you to stay strong through everything." He smiled at her and extended his gloved hand to her. Though there were layers of latex between them, Carol could feel his sincerity as she shook his hand.

"You got it, Dr. J," Carol said smiling at him. It was a relief to have a doctor who genuinely cared. He knew Carol. She was more than just scribbled notes on a patient chart to him. He treated her like a person, something the hospital staff had been lax about. "Hey, doctor, I have a question for you."

"Okay shoot," he said.

"How long do you think I'm gonna be stuck in here?"

"I don't know, Carol," Dr. J answered, shaking his head. "Sorry. It's all dependent on your immune system. Your liver is weak, so my guess is that this is going to be an extremely long recovery."

"Oh," Carol said in a depressed and defeated tone.

"Carol, don't give up on me now. You're here for a reason. Keep fighting until all of this is over."

"I'll try," she said meekly.

"Will, I need you to do something." Carol said over the phone. The reception was poor and she was speaking loudly.

"What's up, Carol?" Will shouted back into his cell phone.

“I need you to bring my laptop to the hospital for me.”

“I don’t think I caught that. Did you say you wanted your laptop?”

“Yeah. I want my laptop here.”

“Why?” Will’s response was garbled.

“What?” Carol shouted.

“Why do you want your laptop?” He answered back.

“I just do, Will. Please just get it from the house and bring it here.”

“I’ll do my best.” Will shouted back through the noise. “I should be able to get it to you tomorrow after work.”

“That would be great!” Carol yelled with all her might. “Thanks, Will.” Carol waited for a response, but there wasn’t any. Will had lost reception completely. Hopefully he heard her.

Carol laid her head back on the pillow and took a few deep breaths. That brief but loud conversation with Will had taken a lot out of her. She closed her eyes and let her weak body rest.

Dr. Ramone came into Carol’s room. The afternoon sun lit him up with a spotlight as he approached Carol’s bed.

“Long time no see,” Dr. Ramone said.

“You’re telling me,” Carol replied. “What’s going on?”

“Not much, Carol. I’m just going to run another panel on you.”

Carol sighed. “What for?”

“I want to check your liver values.”

“When can I have surgery?”

"That's what I'm trying to figure out. I'm hoping to get you in some time in the next couple of weeks depending on those liver values. Could be sooner, could be later. It all depends on how strong your body is."

"Ugh," Carol grunted.

"I know you don't like this. It's the only way. We can't push you, we would put your life in danger."

"I wish you would," Carol mumbled to herself.

"Just be patient, Carol. I'm going to have my resident, Ronnie, come in and take your sample. Okay?"

"Yeah," Carol replied coldly. She lay back on the bed and waited for this new person, Ronnie, to come in and take more of her precious blood.

Dear Alex, I was talking to Dr. Parker. He's the hospital psychiatrist. Anyway, he and I were talking. We were talking about life after death. Is there one? What happens after we die, Alex? I'm really confused. I don't know what to think or what to expect. Could you help me out? I don't know how, but just something, anything to show me. It's an answer that I really need and to get it from you would mean more than anything. Sorry for the strange request. I hope that I hear from you somehow. Thanks, baby. I love you!

Chapter 11

“Here’s your laptop,” Will said. “You would not believe the hoops they made me jump through just to get this to you.”

“Thanks, Will. I appreciate it. I’m sure it wasn’t easy. God forbid someone should just visit me without it becoming a production. I can imagine they gave you hell for this.”

“Yeah, a little. But I reminded them that you’re my boss and I couldn’t lose my job because they wouldn’t let me get a computer to you.” He chuckled.

Carol laughed. “Nice. Thanks, Will. Now they’re going to think I’m some kind of dictator boss.”

“Anyone of them who has spent any time around you knows better than that.” Will smiled under his mask. Carol could see it in his eyes. After a moment, Will’s face dropped. “I hate to run, but I have to get home to Robyn.”

“Oh. Okay,” Carol sounded disappointed. “Wait, how is Sugar? Is Robyn still happy with her?”

“Oh... yeah. In fact, that’s where I’m going. I’m going home so that she and I can take Sugar out for a little walk.”

“Will, it’s about ten degrees outside. Where are you walking her?”

“Just around. A little walk. I know it’s cold, but they’ve both been cooped up for so long, that they’re going stir crazy. We won’t be out for long, but hopefully just a few minutes will do them both a world of good.”

Carol stared at Will for a few moments. “Alright. If you say so. Give Sugar a kiss for me.”

"Will do, Carol." Will softly replied before he turned and walked out of her room.

"Stir crazy. That's bullshit. If they want to go stir crazy, they should try this fucking awful solitary confinement." Carol said to herself.

"Good news," Dr. Ramone said as he entered the room. "Your liver values are improving."

"That is good news." Carol said excitedly. "When can I have the surgery?"

"Hold on. They're improving, but you're not out of the woods yet. The surgeon, Dr. J and I all agree that your values need to hold steady within the normal range before we begin anything. You still have some waiting to do."

"I am sick of laying here for nothing, Dr. Ramone. I just lie here and get injected several times a day and I have things sucked out of me at least once a day. All I feel is pain, so then I get shot up with more morphine. I just want to get this over with." Carol said emphatically.

"I completely understand your frustration," Dr. Ramone gently answered. "I know this less than ideal. But there's nothing we can do. You're a risky case, Carol. You're going to have to trust us to do what's in your best interest."

Carol glared at him. She wasn't sure she should trust him. She wondered if he really did have her best interest at heart. Dr. Ramone stood awkwardly in front of her.

After a few moments of silence, the door opened. Both Carol and Dr. Ramone turned. Dr. Parker came in.

"That's my cue. We'll talk more about this after tomorrow's blood results." Dr. Ramone nodded at Dr. Parker and left Carol's room.

"How are you today?" Dr. Parker asked as he sat down.

"Great. Just great," Carol sarcastically replied.

"How are you?" Tyrone quietly asked as he approached Carol. It was odd that Tyrone was visiting alone, but Carol enjoyed the quiet. The visits with all the family members were so draining to her. Visits with individual family members were far more tolerable.

"Alright I guess, Tyrone. Days just keep coming and going and nothing happens. My life is wasting away. There's no point, no meaning to my life here."

"Yes there is."

"Then tell me. What is it, Tyrone? Do you know? Do you know what purpose I can serve laying here, completely unable to do anything?" Carol's frustration was palpable.

"That's something you'll need to figure out. You wouldn't be here if there wasn't a purpose."

Carol sighed at Tyrone's cliché. "How's Candace?" She asked after a few silent moments.

"Good. It's getting more difficult for her to get around. She's really excited. The baby is due so soon."

"That's great," Carol said quietly.

"She misses you." Tyrone said.

"Tell her I miss her too."

"I sure will," Tyrone smiled. "Is there... uhhhh... anything I can do, Carol? Anything you need from me or anything?"

"No," Carol answered. She was confused by Tyrone's question. "I'm fine, thanks."

"Oh, okay." Tyrone replied. The two sat in awkward silence for several moments. "Well... uhhh... it's getting late.

I'd best be on my way."

"Okay," Carol replied. She hated the fact that everyone else could leave whenever they wanted, but she was stuck in this dungeon. "I guess I'll see you around, Tyrone."

"Yeah," he answered brightly. He looked at her one last time and then left the room. The door shut and Carol was once again left to the deafening silence of her hospital room.

Carol was becoming used to nights of sleeplessness. Her body was becoming far too dependent on the morphine and other drugs to keep her comfortable. Since her pain was severe enough to keep her from sleeping, Carol decided to open her laptop.

After it booted up and picked up a Wi-Fi signal, Carol went on the internet. She went to Google. In the search bar, she slowly typed in "life after death beliefs." She paused for a moment. Was she really going to do this? Yes, she decided. She needed answers. She then clicked on the search button and waited to see the results.

"It was good to see you again, Carol." Candace said as she pushed herself out of the chair. It was the first time she had been back to visit in days. Carol was thrilled to see her.

"Yeah, you too, C." Carol hated to see Candace leave, but she knew that everyone else had lives outside of this hospital, unlike her.

"I hate to run, but I have to do some reading for work before this day slips away."

"Slips away," Carol mumbled to herself. Everything was slipping away, it seemed.

“I understand. I’ll see you soon.” Carol said, looking up at Candace.

Candace smiled down at her. “Yeah,” she said before turning and leaving Carol’s room.

“Slips away,” Carol said softly as she gazed out the window. She watched the day slip into the night. Despite various healthcare people coming and going; injecting Carol with more medications and continually monitoring her vital signs, Carol’s eyes were fixated on the black sky and the silver moon.

As the words “slips away” continually played in her head, Carol was reminded of Led Zepplin’s *Tangerine*. She quietly sang as she stared out the window. “*Measuring a summer's day, I only finds it slips away to grey, The hours, they bring me pain. I was her love, she was my queen, And now a thousand years between.*” The melody played endlessly in Carol’s mind as the night ticked away. She sang quietly for hours on end, until the final lines became too emotional for her to sing any longer. Slowly Carol turned her head away from the window as tears rolled down her cheeks. She closed her eyes and prayed that peace and sleep would finally wash over her.

Chapter 12

The sun was just beginning to peer over the tops of the larger buildings in the hospital's complex. Carol hardly slept. Tangerine continued to play in her mind. Never before had she wanted silence in her head as much as she did at this moment.

She grabbed her journal and she turned to the next blank page. She sighed, thinking about what she would write. After a few contemplative moments, she took her pen and wrote, "*Thinking how it used to be, Does she still remember times like these? To think of us again? And I do.*"

Carol gently closed the book shut and placed it under her pillow, hoping that she could somehow find solace in the written words. She closed her eyes once again and tried to let her mind drift so she could finally get some rest.

Carol was flipping through the channels, when something caught her eye. The Princess Bride was on. Her heart began to race, she felt slightly queasy, and her vision was blurred from the tears that had yet to be released. No sooner had she stopped to watch the movie then Byron walked in.

"What are you watching?" His voice was somewhat muffled from his mask, and he wasn't looking directly at Carol as he walked in. Once fully inside the room, he turned and saw the movie. "Ah, The Princess Bride. Alex's favorite movie."

Carol was silent for a few moments. She took a few deep

breaths to fight back the tears. "She was wrong, you know." Carol's voice was so soft it was nearly inaudible.

"What did you say?" Byron turned and asked her.

"Alex. She was wrong, Byron. She listened to this movie. She believed it. Whole-heartedly believed this crap. She always told me that not even death could stop true love because of this movie. This stupid, lying, fucking movie. That's not true, Byron. It's just not true." Carol began sobbing.

Byron hesitantly approached her bed. "How do you know that's not true, Carol?" He gently asked.

"I'm still alive and she's gone. Death stopped our true love." Carol sobbed for several moments.

Byron stood over her awkwardly, unsure how he could console her. "But, you still love her and she always loved you. Nothing can ever stop that, Carol." He replied gently.

"Death stops everything." Carol said, her voice was filled with pain and anger.

There is a world going on all around me that doesn't care whether I join in the chaos or just slip away into death. It will keep going, no matter what I do. So, would it even really matter? Do I even really matter?

Carol closed the black cover to her journal. Those thoughts were so true, and so painful. She began to wonder if anything really mattered any more. Carol looked out the window. The night was as black as her book and her thoughts. Determined to find a purpose in her existence, she looked up to see the stars twinkling in the clear winter night.

"Did you know that the ancient Egyptians believed that

your heart was weighed against the feather of justice? If your heart is lighter than the feather, you go to heaven, well, their concept of heaven. If your heart is heavier, you're devoured by a monster and you live in oblivion for eternity." Carol was speaking quite clearly despite the fact that her medicinal regimen had been increased substantially.

"Where did you hear that?" Dr. Parker asked.

"I was a history minor in college. My father taught me the importance of history. Now, it's time I actually use it."

Dr. Parker shifted in his seat. "Okay, what do you think about that?"

"I like the idea of the feather of justice. But, if you make it to heaven, you continue whatever work you did here on Earth. I don't want to be fixing computers in heaven. Maybe being eaten by the monster is the best bet for me."

Dr. Parker didn't respond to Carol's comment. "What other beliefs are out there?" He asked.

"From what I've read, it seems the Greeks kind of invented a torturous and torment filled hell. They had the idea of being tortured if you're a bad person. For example, Tantalus was forced to be permanently hungry and thirsty. He sat under a fruit tree and near some water, both of which were just out of reach. That's pretty cruel."

"I take it you don't like that," Dr. Parker said without any hint of emotion.

"The Elysian Fields, their version of heaven, sounds nice. But I'd hate to be permanently hungry and thirsty and to have what I want or need right in front of me but out of reach."

"That makes sense," he responded emotionlessly.

"In ancient Rome, life was considered a punishment and death was freedom."

"What do you make of that, Carol?"

"I can easily agree that life is hell. I hope that death does bring freedom. I'm so sick of the darkness, pain and misery in life. I just want to be free of it all."

"What about modern religions?"

"Well, any form of Christianity would send me straight to hell simply because I loved another woman. I don't get it. Love is love, no matter who the person is, right? Apparently, some faiths believe we can turn off our emotions and ignore our hearts."

"I wouldn't say that, Carol."

"Why not? Are you one of them? Do you want to condemn me to hell simply because the person I loved was a woman? What about love thy neighbor and all that bullshit?"

"I wasn't saying that, Carol." He gently replied. "I understand. Let's face it, the gay community faces a lot of obstacles because people react out of fear. A lot of those fearful people use their religions to defend their actions and words. I don't think they are actually against love. It might be that they are afraid or possibly even envious of a love that can endure such social scorn.

"Straight white Christians are basically well accepted in our American society. It's easy for them to forget what hardships other races and groups of people have endured because it was never their problem. Perhaps people who are different from them, people who can remain stoic in the face of social adversity remind them that there is more to life than whatever is in their sphere of knowledge. Perhaps they're jealous because they know they couldn't do what you do. Maybe they're not strong enough to stand up for themselves in the same way you and Alex did, for example." He paused to watch Carol. "What do you think? Think it's possible?"

Carol took a deep breath. "I never thought of it that way. If people are afraid, though, why do they act out in such anger and hatred? It just doesn't make sense to me. If I'm afraid of something, I either try to find out information about it or I just leave it alone."

"Some people just don't know how to act, let alone be kind, when they're afraid." Dr. Parker said gently. This was the most compassion he had shown Carol during her entire stay in the hospital. "So, what do you think now? How do you feel about religion and facing death?"

Carol struggled to keep her eyes focused on him. She could no longer fight the extra medications Shelby had given her right before Dr. Parker arrived. "I guess I'm as ready as I'll ever be. Nobody really knows anyway."

Carol could hear Dr. Parker say something, but she didn't understand him. She felt a little droplet of drool trickle down her chin. The room became a swirl of colors and she finally succumbed to the sleep that her body so desperately needed.

Carol blinked several times as she slowly woke up. Someone was coming in, but she couldn't discern who it was yet. As the person approached and Carol's eyes cleared, she could see that it was Erin.

"Erin," Carol yawned. "Long time no see."

"Yeah, I know." Erin said softly as she cautiously sat on the edge of Carol's bed. She seemed to have difficulty moving in the protective suit. "How are you?"

"Tired."

"I've been looking over your medical records."

Carol looked at Erin's eyes. She could barely see them over the surgical mask.

"Carol, you're on a lot of meds. You're not healing quickly. I'm worried about you."

"Erin, I'm an AIDS patient who tried to OD on her meds and then totaled her car. I'm not going to be doing well. I want to get the surgeries over with, but whatever. I'm going to die anyway and probably soon."

"Don't say that," Erin cried out.

"Why not?" Carol quietly asked.

"Carol, you're too young. I know you can get through this. You just need to stay positive."

"Tell me something about yourself, Erin."

"What?" Erin asked.

"Tell me something about yourself. Anything."

"Why?"

"Because I'm sick of only talking about medical stuff, waiting for surgeries and why I shouldn't talk about dying."

Erin was silent for a moment. "Well... uhhhh... I like to make small sculptures out of clay. It's my hobby. It's a good break from the stress and depression of working at the home."

"Wow, that's really nice. That's different from what I expected to hear." Carol whispered, "How long have you been sculpting?"

"Just for a few years now. I'm still quite new at it, but I enjoy it," Erin said meekly.

Carol didn't respond. It was nice to hear about Erin's hobby, but it really wasn't terribly important to her. Finally Carol blurted out the question she had really wanted to ask, "Erin, you're so quiet and gentle. How do you put up with someone as loud and aggressive as Byron?"

Erin sat silently for a moment. Her surprise was painted all over her face. "Byron isn't as bad as you think, Carol. He's really a teddy bear. He's just very protective. Since he was a kid, he had to protect both of his sisters and even his mother to some extent. He's a protector and he refuses to let anyone he loves get hurt. It's really quite admirable."

"But doesn't Buddhism teach peace?" Carol asked.

“Yes, it does. And there is peace. We both have peace. We have peace in our hearts from happiness and from knowing our roles in our marriage and in society.”

“Byron wasn’t very peaceful with me when it came to me and Alex was first diagnosed.”

Erin sighed. “I know. Trust me. Between Alex, Candace and me, Byron was ripped a new one many times. He just didn’t know how to react. He felt like he had failed at protecting his sister.”

Carol looked down at her hands. They were so small and there were wires and tubes coming out all around both of them. Carol thought her hands, like the rest of her, were ugly. “Do you think I failed her?”

“No. not at all, Carol. You gave so much more to Alex than anyone ever could have. You didn’t know. You would never have intentionally hurt Alex. We all know that, Byron included. Neither he, nor you, failed at protecting or loving Alex. Got it?”

Still staring at her weak, wrinkly, IV-ridden, ugly hands, Carol finally mumbled, “Yeah.”

“Carol, I can’t even begin to imagine what you’re going through, but please know that we love you. We all love you, Byron included.”

Carol looked up and could see Erin was smiling under her mask. “Thanks,” Carol murmured.

Erin stayed in the chair for a moment. She nodded at Carol and then rose and slowly walked out of Carol’s room. She gently closed the door behind her. It was apparent she didn’t want to strain Carol with a too-long visit.

Chapter 13

Carol continually hummed the melody to *Tangerine*. She could not get the song out of her mind, it was fitting though. Led Zepplin songs had a way of bringing Carol solace, so she quietly sang along contentedly.

As she continued to sing, Shelby walked into her room. Carol quickly stopped, embarrassed.

"Don't stop on account of me. I think you have a pretty voice. I've been listening for a little while now. I figured I'd come in early before the chaos of the day begins."

Carol looked up at the clock on the wall. It was early. "Why are you here?" She asked. She couldn't understand why anyone would want to come to her room any more than absolutely necessary.

"Can I ask you a question?" Shelby answered Carol with a question.

Carol replied quizzically, "okay?"

"What do you think about?"

Carol stared at Shelby. Her light eyes twinkled despite the layers of protection that stood between the two women.

"You're here day in and day out. You don't get to go home. What do you think about while we're poking and prodding you or while you're just lying here all alone? You seem so sad all the time," Shelby said softly.

"I've been happier." Carol smiled weakly. "I don't know, Shelby. I think about all kinds of things, I guess."

"You don't watch much TV, you don't read. Do you think about your business? Your family? What life will be like when you get out of here?"

"You make it sound like a prison," Carol chuckled lightly. "No, I don't watch too much TV. It's all the same, really. Blood, gore and depressing news. There's only so much of that a person can take, you know?"

"I don't know why I don't read, I should. I have a great collection of historical books from my dad. I should read those again. It would beat staring out the window endlessly."

"I'll bet," Shelby said. She sat down in the chair opposite Carol's bed. "Do you think about work?"

"No. Not at all. The company is in good hands. It's no longer a part of my life, so I have no need to worry about it."

"But you'll be working again once all of this is over. Won't you?"

"I doubt it, Shelby. The company has already been signed over to my good friend, Will. He's a good man and a smart technician. I trust him. And should I be lucky enough to get out of here alive, I'm sure he'd hire me back." Carol laughed.

Shelby smiled and laughed under her mask. She noticed that Carol had a beautiful smile. It was nice to see it for a change.

"I think about all kinds of things. I think about my dog. I think about my life and the way it was before everything happened. I think about my dad. I think about my two dead best friends."

"That's pretty morbid, Carol. Why do you focus so much on people who have passed?"

"I don't know. Maybe I hope they're still with me or that I will see them again. I don't want them to be forgotten. There's a lot I think about when I think about them. I mean, I wonder where they are and where I'm headed when I die."

Shelby quietly sighed. "I wish you'd stop talking like that,

Carol. You'll get through all of this. You are an incredible woman. This is a mere bump in the road for someone like you."

Carol blushed. "Thanks, Shelby."

Just then, Shelby's watched beeped. "Well, that was way too short. It's time for your morning meds. Let me go get those and I'll be right back."

"Okay," Carol sighed. Yet another day was starting, another carbon copy of all the previous days, and a template for all the days yet to come.

"Judaism doesn't seem to talk much about what happens after we die. It's not the main focus of their religion, which is kind of a nice reprieve." Carol nodded. "I did see that in some Jewish beliefs, though, good people are reunited with their loved ones. Bad people are cut off. But they believe everyone has a soul and that soul is a part of God's essence. Evil people are still punished in some kind of hell. It's kind of interesting."

"So what do you think of that belief?" Once again Carol and Dr. Parker discussed life after death. Carol didn't like being so morbid, but she knew that her circumstances forced her to think in this capacity.

"I'm not sure yet. just read that last night. I want to think about it, all of it. I'm sure something in there somewhere makes sense somehow."

"Okay, fair enough. What about Islam?"

"Well, from what I understand, there is a day of judgment. The dead are brought back to life and everyone is judged. Some people go to hell and besides burning in the fire, they have a figurative fire in their heart. If that happens, basically they are in a state of emotional unrest and are tortured emotionally as much as physically tortured. The holy go to paradise and they have complete happiness and peace in their hearts."

"What category do you fall into?" Dr. Parker asked.

"I'll burn in hell, according to them. Sodomy or homosexuality is considered extremely amoral and inexcusable. They don't believe that homosexuality is biological. So, I'm basically screwed." Carol sighed heavily and looked out her window.

"I'm sorry," Dr. Parker uttered. "Let's change gears. What else do you want to talk about today, Carol?"

"I don't. I want to draw, or read or do a crossword puzzle. I'm sick of the routine here. I don't want to have any more morbid conversations. I want some semblance of normalcy in here. It may seem impossible to do so, but I want to try."

"Okay, that's fair. I can understand that." Dr. Parker seemed more caring to Carol. "You know, I do have a crossword puzzle from today's paper in my office. Would you like it?"

Carol stared back at him in surprise. He was offering her something, something she'd actually enjoy. "If you don't mind," she replied meekly.

"No, not at all. Let me go get it. I'll be back in a few minutes."

"Okay, thanks." Carol smiled as Dr. Parker walked out of the room. It was only a crossword puzzle, but it was a great gift that he was extending to her.

Dear Alex, I couldn't sleep last night. I hardly sleep at all anymore. Between the pain and boredom, this isn't living. It's even worse because you're not here.

Last night, I started looking for song lyrics. I looked at

Unforgettable, like when you sang that to me at Byron's wedding. Of course, I also found some good old Hendrix, Floyd, The Who, Joplin, The Doors and Led Zep songs. No matter what song it was, though, I thought of you. It wasn't bad thinking of you; it just hurts so much. It's a constant reminder that you're not here. I don't know if I was trying to forget you or find lyrics that mirrored my pain, but I kept looking. Eventually, I found some new song lyrics that made me think of you and me. And even all this shit that's going on right now.

First, there is a Melissa Ethridge song. I've never heard this song before, but the lyrics are touching. Well, at least they were last night while I was all drugged up and unable to sleep. Anyway, let me tell you about this song. The chorus starts with, "There is no mountain that I can't climb/For you I'd swim through the rivers of time." That is so true. I could do anything with you and I would do anything for you. I would do everything that I could just to be with you again. I would do it in the past, and I'd still do it, baby. I would do anything for you.

In my search, I even found songs from foreign musicians. Can you believe that? I almost dismissed them, but then I saw that one European band had "Without you I cannot be." When I read that line, I was simply floored. It was as if they had gotten into my head and wrote that. It is so true for me, Alex. I cannot live, I cannot exist without you. That's how I ended up here. My heart died when you died, Alex. I am not living. I cannot be me without you. They also had, "And I, I only wait for you." Seeing you again is what I live for. Every minute of my life has been spent waiting for you. And I don't regret it, Alex. I'll always wait for you.

Oh here's another good one. This one was from Lenny Kravitz, I think. I'm not even sure this one needs explanation. It's just so perfect. "Ain't no sunshine when she's gone. It's not warm when she's away. Ain't no sunshine when she's gone, and she's always gone too long anytime she goes away." Perfect, huh? Looking back at these, they almost seem redundant. Maybe I'm a redundant person. I don't know. These just all mirror how I feel, Alex. Look at this one, "'Cause I'm broken when I'm lonesome. And I don't feel right when you're gone away." I haven't felt right in ages. Without you, I'm nothing. I've been broken since you've been gone, my love.

"I can't let her go. 'Cause I need the love she gives to me." This one is really true, too. I can't let you go. How could I ever let go of the best thing to ever happen to me? You were the one person who truly accepted me and loved me just as I am. You were the only person who made me genuinely happy. You gave me more than I ever could have imagined. I can't let that go. And I do need the love you gave to me. That was more important to me than air. I could go without food, water, shelter, air... you name it. As long as I had your love. That has always been the most important thing to me.

Lastly, I found this one. For whatever reason, we've been separated. But that does not change how I feel about you. Nothing can ever change that. "I will always love you no matter what. No matter where you go or what you do." Perfect song lyrics for us. That is exactly how I feel, Alex. I will always love you no matter what or where you go or what more can happen to us. To me, I guess I should say. Regardless, I will always love you with every inch of my being.

You know, Alex, as great as love is, it also just plain sucks. It's hard. It devours us. It tears us apart from the inside out. It just hurts us. Love hurts so freaking much. Loving my father hurt. It hurt because he died and far too soon. Loving Ed like he was a brother to me hurt. It hurt because he wanted more than just our friendship and it hurt when he died. Loving Marlene as a friend hurt. I loved her because we never got in each other's way. We were perfect roommates. Then we went our separate ways. It hurt the most when I thought I had just been reunited with her and then she died, too. Love just hurts. Everyone I love ends up hurting me because they die, leaving me with the pain.

Loving and losing you hurt, too, sweetheart. Loving you was the greatest thing I have ever experienced. But, it also hurt far too much. Losing you was worse than losing my home, my family, whatever you can think of. Loving you was the greatest part of my life; losing you was the worst. My heart may beat on, but my soul is dead. My soul died along with you, Alex. I just miss you so much, honey. I just want you back. I'm trying to fill my days with crossword puzzles or books, but nothing will ever fill the void that was created when you left.

I love you, Alex. I always have and I always will. Please don't ever question that. Know that you are my life, my love, my reason for living. I am not whole without you. I love you, Alex. Can you hear me? I love you.

"Here are some of the books you wanted, Carol." Byron said dumping a large pile of thick, hard cover books on the night stand next to Carol's bed.

"They actually let you bring them?" Carol was surprised.

"It wasn't easy, but when Shelby heard what it was she made sure they didn't give me any trouble."

"It was her idea." Carol smiled.

"I'm glad," Byron smiled back. "I think these will be good for you. I'm thrilled she talked you into it."

"Beats just laying here doing nothing, right?"

Byron looked away. "I'm just thrilled to see you happy."

"I'm as happy as I can be considering the circumstances, I guess." Carol said.

"Well, that's a damn good start, Carol. I hope you enjoy these."

"I will," Carol said. She was smiling broadly.

"What do you want?" Dr. Parker asked. "Right this very instant. Tell me the first thing that comes to mind."

"Freedom." Carol hesitated before blurting out her answer.

"Freedom. What is freedom to you?"

"Not being here," Carol mumbled.

"I know you don't want to be in here. You've been here quite a while. Describe what freedom would mean to you right now. We can't go back in time and have Alex. It's for the present. What would freedom look like right now?"

Carol leaned her head to the side as she thought about freedom. "Well," she started, "I think I would be back on one of those back country roads where I taught Alex how to drive a stick. It would be a beautiful, sunny day and I would be in the GTO without a care in the world. Being outside and being in the car, that's freedom to me." Carol paused, imagining what freedom would feel like. "I think I would just be driving around when something like The Doors' Roadhouse Blues begins to play on the radio," she continued.

"At first, I would simply smile and enjoy the moment. I don't think it would take me long before I tried to sing along with the deep base of Jim Morrison. As the song picks up and the harmonica screams, I know that I wouldn't be able to resist swaying to the southern rock/blues song. I'm sure I'd begin drumming on the steering wheel of my father's GTO in no time, too.

"Then, something like *Smoke on the Water* would play. Who doesn't love that song? I would blast that music as loud as I could and just let myself get lost in that incredible guitar riff.

"And it would just be one incredible song after another.

Like Led Zeplin's Rock and Roll, or Kiss the Sky by Hendrix or Santana's Oye Como Va. Or maybe Jumpin' Jack Flash by the Stones or even something like Comfortably Numb by Pink Floyd. Any of those great classic rock songs where you just get swept away and you're just completely happy. The great music just wouldn't stop and I could just drive wherever I wanted to. That's freedom."

Dr. Parker smiled. "And what would freedom like that do for you, emotionally?"

Carol didn't even think before she answered. "Being in the car and hearing that music brings back wonderful childhood memories of me and my dad. I'd be smiling a really big smile. I would be genuinely happy. Though I'm not much of a dancer, I'd bob and weave and dance in my seat like a fool." Carol smiled a bright smile.

Dr. Parker smiled back at Carol. She was running away with her imagination, completely forgetting her surroundings for once.

"I'd be like a kid again." Carol paused while a large smile was painted across her face. "In fact, my 'inner child' would be completely unleashed as I sang and danced without a care in the world."

Still smiling, Carol looked up at Dr. Parker.

"Sounds wonderful," he whispered.

Nate walked in quietly. It was towards the end of visiting hours and he couldn't be sure Carol would be awake. As he slipped into her room he saw her reading one of her thick history books.

"Hi Carol," he said gently.

Carol looked up from her book. "Hi Nate." Her voice sounded weak. She was losing weight, too. Her pale skin had lost what little color it did have. Yet, Carol smiled brightly at her dear friend.

"How are you?" He asked as he maneuvered his way through the room in the over-sized bunny suit.

"I'm here. What are you doing here so late?"

"I just got off work. I thought I should stop by. I haven't seen you enough. I haven't been a really good friend."

"You've been fine, Nate. No worries," Carol said as she placed the book down on the small stand next to her bed. "So, what's going on in the real world?"

"Can I ask you a question?" Nate's voice was muffled behind the surgical mask, but Carol understood him.

"Yeah."

"Carol, why did you do this? I mean, hell, I don't know what I mean. I lost Aaron and it hurt like hell. I hated being in the empty house. I hated my life without him, but I couldn't imagine doing what you did."

Carol sighed heavily. "I guess we all deal with loss differently, Nate. The empty house sucks. It's eerie and lifeless. There's nothing there. There's no one to watch a baseball game with me or share a meal with. Alex was my purpose. She was the reason I did everything. If she wasn't there, what was I supposed to do? Besides, it was my fault she died."

"It's not your fault she died. You know better than that." For a normally timid man, Nate was speaking as sternly as he could. "I know how much you adored her, but think of all the good you could have done in her honor."

"I tried that, Nate." Carol defensively replied. "I left a message on Byron's phone a few days after the funeral. I wanted to start some kind of charity or fund or something. He never called me back, so it never got started."

"So you're going to blame things on other people now?"

Carol was stunned. "Wait, what?"

"Just because Byron didn't call you back didn't mean you couldn't have done it on your own. You could have asked us in group to help you."

Carol was silent as she absorbed Nate's words. She had never thought of those options. She had given up too easily. She drew in a few deep breaths. "You're right," she said quietly.

"It's not too late, you know." He gently replied.

"It's not?" Carol looked at him, confused.

"We were talking about it at group last night. That's what made me decide to come over. What would you like us to do, Carol? You name it and we'll get something started for you."

Carol felt overwhelmed. The generosity of the group was unsurpassed. Tears began to well up in her eyes as she thought of all the good that could be done in Alex's honor. A few tears escaped down her face before Carol was able to speak. "I want... an AIDS charity or fund. But not just for research or treatment. I want something that will help young girls on the street who are HIV/AIDS positive and don't have a way of turning their lives around the way Alex did. This way we can reach the AIDS community and we can help girls whose lives are as desolate as Alex's once was." Carol paused to think. It didn't take long before she carefully nodded her head yes. "Yes, that's what I want, Nate."

"Okay. I'll tell Juanita at the next group meeting and we'll get something set up."

Carol smiled through her tears. "Thanks, Nate." Her voice cracked.

Dear Alex, Why is life so hard? People die, medical bullshit, constant changes. It's all too much for me to take in.

Impeccable

Why does life have to be so full of pain? Why can't it be simpler and happier? Why can't you and I still be together? Why do I have to be in this bed with a million lines and shit coming in and going out of me? Why is life like this? It just plain sucks.

I miss you. And I love you. Love, Carol.

Chapter 14

"Good morning, Carol." Dr. Parker said as he came into her room. He had a small canvas, a couple of paint brushes and a small dish of paints. "Today, we're going to do something different."

"What are we doing?" Carol asked cautiously. This was very different from Dr. Parker's norm.

"I want you to paint. I want you to paint your idea of paradise. Perhaps a dream that you and Alex shared. Something that's special. A place that brings you peace and joy. It can be real or fake. You can have landscapes, people, and animals, whatever you want. This is your painting. Your version of paradise."

"But I can't paint," Carol weakly protested.

"Have you ever tried?"

"Well, no."

"Then how do you know? Besides, this isn't for an art contest. It's my version of art therapy. I think it might help you. Plus it's a nice change of pace. Just give it a try."

"Okay," Carol agreed.

Dr. Parker called Shelby in. A few moments later, Shelby walked into Carol's room in her usual get-up.

"Would you mind helping her with her various lines as she paints, Shelby?"

"No, not at all, Dr. Parker. That's no problem."

"Perfect! Thanks. I'll be back in a bit to see what you've painted." Dr. Parker set everything down on a little rolling tray and walked out of Carol's room.

Shelby began rearranging Carol's IV lines, her bed and all of the supplies so that Carol wouldn't have any difficulty as she painted. Once everything was set up, Shelby handed the canvas and brushes over to Carol.

"So, what are you going to paint?" Shelby sweetly asked.

"Dr. Parker wants me to paint my picture of paradise, or something like that."

"So what are you thinking of?"

"I love big, rolling green hills. Alex and I always liked the country side. And maybe a creek. You know: pretty, nature-y things."

Carol carefully guided the brush over the canvas to start the rolling hills from her imagination. As her hand lightly glided over the canvas board, Carol let herself get swept up in the moment. "Alex and I loved just driving around the countryside for hours on end. We would just drive and sing together. It's how I taught her to drive a stick," she whispered as she painted.

Shelby deftly handled all of Carol's various lines as her arms moved with her careful and detailed painting.

It wasn't long before the canvas revealed a bright, sunny day. The sky was a perfect powder blue. The rolling green hills were lush and luxurious. Trees flourished all over the hills. Beautiful, delicate flowers peppered the country side. A small creek ran along the bottom edge of the canvas.

"That is a perfect sky, Carol. Not one cloud," Shelby said softly.

"No." Carol replied. She didn't need to say any more. Carol was sure that Shelby understood what she meant.

Carol dipped her brush in the black paint and began to paint over one of the green hills.

"What are you doing?" Shelby asked in shock.

"Alex and I sometimes talked about riding horses. Neither of us had ever ridden a horse before. But it would be great if we could ride horses together in this scene."

Shelby quietly watched Carol paint. Carol was very focused and detail-oriented. Her brush delicately touched the canvas, each stroke was intentional.

After several moments of silence, there were silhouettes

of Carol and Alex both riding horses over one of the hills.

"It's beautiful," Shelby whispered.

Carol was finishing a few minor details when Dr. Parker walked back in. "So, what do we have?" He asked as he came around Carol's bed. "Wow. Carol, you paint very well. This is beautiful."

Carol blushed a little. "Thanks."

"Tell me about it," Dr. Parker said.

"Well, I don't know where it is. Maybe Ireland or Scotland. Or maybe somewhere in the United States. I don't know. It's just somewhere where there are endless rolling green hills and creeks, and someplace Alex and I can ride horses together."

"Sounds perfect to me," Dr. Parker said approvingly.

"Okay, Carol. The worst part will be this local anesthetic. It's going to sting when I give it to you." The plastic surgeon Dr. Ramone sent in told her. Carol wasn't interested when he told her his name.

The wound on her face never healed. There was still a large open cut across her cheek, just under her eye. The plastic surgeon was brought in to clean it up and suture it closed. Though it was not a life saving surgery, Dr. Ramone assured Carol that it was indeed progress. Carol simply went through the motions as she had no other choice. She knew it really needed to be done. She sighed and looked over at the stranger who was about to fix her face.

This doctor, whose dark eyes sat high above the surgical mask, came at Carol's face with a needle. Scared, Carol flinched and closed her eyes. She could feel the needle pierce her skin and it did burn as he pushed the plunger. She felt the medication being absorbed by the nerves and tissue and then it stopped.

Carol opened her eyes again only to see him approaching with another needle. She quickly shut her eyes and waited for the sting. Once again, Carol felt pain as the fluid left the syringe and entered her cheek. The doctor repeated this pattern a few more times. It became slightly more tolerable with each injection.

"I'm going to let this set in and we'll be good to go," the doctor said. He might as well have just been talking to himself. He wasn't even looking at Carol and he didn't seem to be addressing Shelby either. Carol didn't have the energy to respond, but even if she had she wouldn't have known what to say to him. The room was quiet. Shelby stood behind him, silently watching Carol with sympathetic eyes.

Carol took a deep breath as she waited. She didn't feel anything happening. Her face wasn't numb. She felt no difference at all. If she felt nothing, how would this doctor know that the medicine had taken effect?

"Betadine, please." He snapped at Shelby. In utter silence, Shelby handed him sterile gauze pads and a pre-warmed, diluted solution of water and Betadine.

The doctor gently dabbed Carol's face. She watched his hand as it moved across the wound, but she felt nothing. Perhaps the local had taken effect faster than she had anticipated.

After a few rounds of cleaning, he gently pulled on her skin. Carol could see a blurred vision of this man pushing and pulling the skin in various directions while he inspected her face. "Light." He snapped again. From behind his shoulder, Shelby shined a light into Carol's wound. "Hamm. I'm impressed."

"Why?" Carol asked. She was confused. What could have possibly impressed this impersonal doctor?

"There's no necrotic tissue. For a wound that has been open this long, and in an immuno-compromised patient, it's not uncommon to see the tissue just die. Your blood flow has been good, the tissue isn't necrotic. It's actually granulating, but very slowly. We're going to help with that."

"Uhhh... okay." Carol didn't know what else to say.

The doctor turned away from her and muttered something to Shelby. After a few silent moments, he turned back around with needle holders and suture material to stitch the wound up.

Carol closed her eyes. The thought of watching him stitch her back up made her nauseas. She tried to focus on her breathing to calm herself. Suddenly, Carol felt a slight pinch that she wasn't expecting. "Oooh," she mumbled.

"Sorry," Shelby whispered compassionately.

The doctor remained silent as he continued. Carol could feel light pinching as he continued to close the gash with the sutures. Carol kept her eyes closed. She tried to focus on her breathing as he worked, but it was difficult. This seemed to take forever. Just when she thought he was done, she felt another pinch. She wondered when this stupid ordeal would finally be over.

After an indefinite amount of time, Carol heard the doctor's chair squeak. Hesitantly, she opened her eyes. He was leaning back, looking at her face while Shelby continued to shine the light on it.

He said nothing for a few moments while he simply stared at Carol. "Looks pretty good. I think I'm done here. Thank you, Shelby." The doctor didn't even look at Shelby or acknowledge Carol as he rose from the chair and left the room.

"Wow that was weird." Carol didn't even realize that she voiced her thoughts aloud.

"Dr. Hollenbacher?" Shelby asked.

Carol jolted into reality and realized that she had accidentally spoken her mind about the impersonal doctor.

"Yeah, sorry about that," Shelby continued. "He's got the bedside manner of rough toilet paper. He's a good plastic surgeon, though. I'll talk to Dr. Ramone and see what we need to do to take care of it and if there is anything we should do for pain, okay?" Shelby kindly responded.

"Thank you, Shelby."

"No problem, Carol," Shelby was smiling under her mask.

Carol felt like Shelby was the one person helping her keep her sanity in this horrid hospital.

Pausing only briefly, Shelby turned, cleaned up the supplies the plastic surgeon used, and left the room.

Carol sighed heavily. She rolled her head slowly to the side and looked out the window. She couldn't see her reflection. She wondered what changes the doctor made. Did she look more or less like her old self? If she ever got out of this hospital, would she return to life as Carol or as someone different?

Carol sighed, relieved that this latest ordeal was over. She decided to let her mind wander and watched the clouds through the window as another boring, grey day passed by.

Candace walked into the room and something new caught her eye. It was something she hadn't seen before. There was a small painting resting on the table by the wall opposite Carol's bed. "Hey, that's really nice. Where'd you get that?" Candace asked.

"I painted that. Just today, in fact."

"Really? Girl, you got some mad skills. I didn't know you could paint."

"Thanks. Neither did I. It was 'art therapy.'"

"Well, it looks great. Tell me about it." Candace eased herself into the chair near Carol's bed.

"Dr. Parker wanted me to paint something like paradise. A place where I'd be happy. So, I painted a pretty countryside with a creek. It's a beautiful sunny day out, without a single cloud in the sky. And that's Alex and me riding horses through the hills."

Candace looked at the painting for a few minutes. "You know what I love, Carol? I love that you have it so you're both shadowed. No one can tell who is who. You're both on horses, but there's no color. It's just the two of you away from labels. Just the two of you in paradise."

"Yeah," Carol softly replied. "Riding horses: something we both wanted to do."

"I know. And look at you two. You're both so free in this. It's great, Carol."

"Hey Candace, how come you went straight for the fact

that there was no color, we were just shadowed?"

"I don't know. I just like the idea of it being the two of you. It doesn't matter who is who. You're together and you're both happy. Why?"

"I don't know." Carol sighed. "I guess I'm just so used to us being black and white and gay. Just label upon label upon label. We were never just people. We were never just Alex and Carol. We were that interracial lesbian couple. It's nice that you appreciated the fact that it was just us without all that labeling shit."

"I know. I know it was hard. I can't even imagine what you two faced day in and day out. It's hard, I know. I get it. For some reason, people can't just see people as people."

"You're telling me. Hell, look at you and Byron. In the beginning, neither of you were happy with me because I was white and I was another girl."

Candace sighed. "Yeah, you're right. We were way out of line. But we changed, didn't we? You became a part of our family, Carol. It didn't take long for us to stop seeing color or gender. We just saw you for who you really are."

"And who am I really?"

"Huh?" Candace paused to look at Carol in utter confusion. "Carol, where is this coming from?"

"I heard you say that your prayers and special services worked for me when I first got here, but I know how Christianity views lesbians."

"Whoa. Hold on there, girl. I hear what you're saying. But that's not us and you know it. You and Alex were together. Byron married a Buddhist. Look at me, I'm pregnant and Tyrone and I aren't married. We're not like that, Carol. We don't judge."

Carol shot Candace a cynical look. "Not to our faces, anyway."

"It's true and you know it. Neither Byron nor I ever judged you or Alex. We certainly had our concerns because the world isn't very open-minded. But we didn't care about your sexuality. We just saw you as two people in love. That's what you were, Carol, just two people."

Carol shook her head and sighed heavily. “Candace,” she said quietly. “My mother had the audacity to condemn me to hell for being gay. And you know what? My father did everything he could for her and then some. And that bitch cheated on him!”

“What?” Candace asked in shock. She had never heard Carol or Alex say anything about this before.

“Yeah. She had an affair with a neighbor for a little while. I was around ten years old, I think. I don’t even think Dad knew what was going on because he was working so hard. He worked two different jobs to pay off all of my childhood medical bills and to keep food on the table. And my ungrateful mother cheated on him. How the hell can she pass judgment on me when she wasn’t even faithful to my father? I was always faithful to your sister.”

“She can’t,” Candace gently replied. “She had no right to say that.”

“She said that it was my horrible lifestyle that killed my dad and that I deserved to get AIDS.” Tears began racing down Carol’s frail cheeks.

“No. No, that’s not true at all, Carol. No. She’s wrong.”

“How do you know?” Carol looked up at Candace with a child-like innocence in her eyes. The pain from her past still haunted her.

“I know because God doesn’t work like that, Carol. It’s not about who you love. It’s how you treat people. It’s being a person of your word. It’s about who you are as a human being.”

“Who am I as a human being? Who am I? Right now, tell me.”

“You are a beautiful, talented, sweet woman with the biggest heart I have ever seen. You fought constant adversity and you always landed on top. You’re a beautiful woman, Carol. That’s what matters. It’s not about labels or the social feathers you ruffle. God couldn’t care less about that. God cares about you. He cares about how you treat people and what you did with your life. It’s not whether or not you’re gay. God doesn’t work that way, Carol. I promise.”

"I hope you're right, Candace." Carol whispered.

"I am. Trust me. I wish you could see the woman I see."

"I want to see her. I want to see me. Show me."

"What?" Candace was confused.

"I haven't seen my face since before the accident and especially now after the plastic surgery... I want to see myself again."

"Okay," Candace said softly. She went through her purse and took out her compact. She opened it and let Carol look at herself in the tiny mirror.

Carol stared at herself. Her pale skin seemed nearly transparent. Her eyes were dull and sunken. The gash on her cheek was long. The skin puffed around the area where the plastic surgeon had sutured the wound closed. Carol didn't look like herself any more. The various bruises and smaller cuts still remained over her face. This wasn't Carol. This was some sick, ugly woman she was looking at. Carol wasn't sure who was staring back at her in the mirror.

"So this is who you see?" Carol timidly asked. "Look at that woman. Her hair is ugly and ratty. She has this horrible scar." Carol stared into the mirror. She sounded as if she was choking back a sob. "There's still a freaking gap in between my front teeth. Everything about me is imperfect."

"No, Carol. I see a beauty that far surpasses any description. You're just looking at your shell, Carol. You're looking at the battering you took in that car accident and you know that surgery can change that with time. You're much more beautiful than what you're seeing in the mirror. You have an inner beauty, you just have to be willing to see it. You are beautiful. I'll bet God thinks so too." Candace's eyes smiled down at Carol.

Carol looked up at Candace, she was too choked up to speak. All she could do was hope that the young woman was right.

All You Need is Love played on an endless loop in Carol's mind. Unable to ignore the song any longer, Carol reached over and grabbed her journal.

The Beatles tell us that love is all we need, but is that really true? If love was all I ever needed, would I still have ended up here?

Carol put the pen down on the notebook and thought about what she just wrote.

Chapter 15

"Tell me about one of your biggest frustrations in life?" Dr. Parker asked.

Carol paused to think. "Ummm... stereotypes. People assume things. People think they know you, but they don't. It seems like people just assume things about me because they can.

"Can you give me some examples, Carol? What do you think people assume about you?"

"Well..." Carol tried to think. "A lot of people assumed Alex was white or that I was black before they even met us. Even Byron assumed that I was black."

"So people make assumptions about your race?" Dr. Parker was obviously confused.

"Yeah. It shouldn't matter, but it does. I guess people just assumed that I'd be with a white girl and she'd be with a black girl." Carol shrugged. "I know that Byron didn't think a white woman would fall in love with his sister or that she would love a white woman back. He met my mom when he bought the GTO for me. He assumed I was adopted because my mom hated me so much. He didn't believe that a mother could have such hatred for her own child."

"And why does that bother you?"

"People just assume they know me or my story before they even meet me. I don't want people to feel things about me based on what they think they know. I want them to know me, the real me." Carol said vehemently.

"Fair enough. What else do people assume about you?"

"A lot of people have thought I grew up privileged because of my college degree or how big and successful Dawson is. People don't realize how hard I worked to get through college, especially without help from my mother. And it's like no one has any idea of the work that goes into keeping Dawson running and doing so well. It's not easy. And my bank account has never been as big as people would like to think."

"People do assume things from appearances, don't they? You present yourself as a strong, intelligent business woman. You wore good suits and nice clothes, which leads people to think only one thing. You're right, they don't know the story beneath the clothes." Dr. Parker answered sympathetically. "What else, Carol? Tell me something else about what people assume. Perhaps on a level deeper than your clothing or skin color."

Carol concentrated on her breathing as she thought about all of the preconceived notions people made about her over the years. "People have assumed I have AIDS because I'm gay, but, being a lesbian has nothing to do with it. I have AIDS because of a blood transfusion. It wouldn't matter if I was gay, straight, bi, transgender or... whatever. I got AIDS from the transfusion, not because of my sexual orientation."

"Well, let's look at that for a moment, Carol. HIV/AIDS has often been called 'the gay man's disease.' There is definitely a social stigma that links homosexuality and HIV/AIDS, but that seems to affect men more than women." Dr. Parker said.

"Yeah," Carol hesitated. "People forget that you can get it in so many different ways and straight people are also at risk." Carol was sure of herself for once. Her knowledge of the subject impressed Dr. Parker.

"You're right, Carol. It's sad that most Americans aren't even aware of the AIDS plague in Africa, let alone here in their own country. They may see commercials, but the real numbers are elusive. If most Americans were aware of the number of global HIV/AIDS patients, I think they'd be astonished. They'd be even more astonished to find out just how many of those people are straight and had risk factors having nothing to do with their sexual orientation."

"Exactly, Dr. Parker. Look at my life, Ed got AIDS from me and he was straight. He got it when I bit him in self-defense. Marlene got AIDS from her husband who slept with prostitutes. People can get AIDS from anyone. It's not just me; it's not just the gay community ."

"Very well said, Carol. Use your life, your words, and your experiences to help educate others on the reality of HIV/AIDS. Show the world the truth about your disease."

Carol smiled at Dr. Parker. "I will. Thanks."

Dr. Ramone was talking with Shelby as he walked into Carol's room.

"What? How is that possible? Has she been on the PCA at all?"

"No, Dr. Ramone. Just the original protocol and extras PRN."

"That's ridiculous Shelby. I appreciate you telling me about this. Let's just do a PCA and continue to monitor her levels and adjust accordingly."

"Yes, Doctor." Shelby quickly shot a sympathetic look towards Carol before leaving the room.

"What's going on?" Carol asked Dr. Ramone.

"Well, I was just on the phone with Dr. J and we were reviewing your records. I was surprised to see you haven't been on a PCA at all since you've been here. They should have put you on that a while ago."

"A what?"

"PCA, a pump. Basically, it's a controlled, continuous injection of analgesics to keep you more comfortable. It's far better than just getting the morphine and other medications you've been getting and then just getting extra as needed. It's a great way for you to get more, it's better, pain management. Especially if we are able to get you into surgery soon. You'll be on one after that anyway. This way, with your condition, your body has a longer time to adjust to the medications. It will help you over all. It's an effective way to treat a case like yours."

"Okay. Whatever you and Dr. J think is best. It would be nice to be able to actually sleep at night."

"You're not sleeping well, Carol?"

"Not really. I haven't been for a while. Between the pain and being afraid of getting too much morphine, I've just kind of let it go."

"I wish you told me about that sooner, Carol, we could have made things more comfortable for you sooner. I'm glad you're telling me now. Hopefully the PCA will help you all around. Because we're switching you over to it, we will need to keep close tabs on your liver values. Also, the change to the PCA may affect your reaction to the medications. You might feel more tired or not affected at all. Just be sure to tell Shelby how you're feeling on a regular basis so we can adjust everything accordingly, okay?"

"Uhhh... Dr. Ramone, this sounds a bit scary. Am I going to be okay?"

"Don't worry, Carol. It will be fine. It's a change for the better, trust me."

"Okay, Dr. Ramone. If you say so." Carol looked at Dr. Ramone. She knew that neither he nor Dr. J would do anything to jeopardize her. She was still scared. She took in a deep breath and accepted this new regime as best she could.

The bright sunrise woke Carol from her light sleep. With her eyes wide open, she felt thirsty for more information. Carefully, Carol reached over and grabbed her laptop.

Once she was set up, Carol typed in another search for answers about life after death. She scrolled over many of the same pages she previously searched. Something new caught her eye, *Deception of Death*.

"I wonder what that is," Carol whispered to herself. Shelby would be in soon to begin yet another torturous day so Carol hurriedly clicked on the link to read what it had to say.

"Sometimes I just wish I had never been found. I should have been left to bleed out in the car." Carol said in a defeated tone.

"Carol, I haven't heard you talk like this in a while. What's going on?" Dr. Parker sympathetically asked.

Carol sighed. "It's just – this sucks, Dr. Parker. This isn't a life. Here I am, I wanted to die, but I am still alive. All of the pain and hell I was trying to escape has come back and then some. This isn't what I wanted."

Dr. Parker hesitated before speaking. "I'm sure it isn't, Carol. But you need to find out why you're here."

"I don't know. I hate this."

"Maybe you shouldn't think about life in this hospital, Carol. Maybe you need to think about you."

"Me? What about me?"

"Maybe it's not about what you are, but about who you are. Describe yourself in one word."

Carol lay silently in her bed.

After a few minutes, Dr. Parker spoke. "Okay, I'll get you started." He waited a moment. "You are..."

"Imperfect," Carol mumbled.

"Enough."

"Huh?" Carol asked with a puzzled look.

"You are enough, Carol. You. Just as you are. At this very moment, you are enough."

Carol lay silently in her bed.

"You are enough, Carol." Dr. Parker quietly repeated himself.

"Ummm... okay?" She replied weakly.

"You are not imperfect, Carol. If anything, you are impeccable." Dr. Parker replied.

Carol snorted in response.

"You are impeccable, Carol. You need to start seeing the positive things about yourself. You need to stop hating yourself and your life. That's going to be your assignment. Start putting a positive spin on your thoughts."

Carol took a deep breath. "Okay. I'll try."

"Hi Will, it's Carol. I know you're busy. I have a favor to ask. Can you go to my house and grab the brief case out of my office? It's the black one, not the brown one I used to bring to work. The black one has a lot of important personal papers. Also, I need the keys to the GTO and the house. Please bring it with you next time you come by. Thanks, Will. I appreciate it. I'll talk to you later."

Carol hung up. She hoped that Will would be able to come through for her soon.

"I decided something today," Carol said proudly to Dr. Parker.

"What's that, Carol?"

"I've decided that I am not going to research after life beliefs any more."

"What made you decide that?"

"Death is inevitable, Dr. Parker. Everyone dies. Man has come up with all kinds of myths and beliefs about what happens after we die. The human race has tried to find solace by making up stories to show that our existence here has a purpose. But, they're all stories. It's all mythology. All religions claim to have it right, but no one knows for certain. Why should I waste my time trying to figure out something that I have no control over?"

"You don't feel you have any control, Carol?"

"No. Nobody does, not about that. Whatever it is, it is. I have no idea. And no matter what I think, my beliefs won't change the final outcome."

"That is bold thinking. You're right that people have always been searching for answers from various belief systems. Most people are afraid to go into an unknown situation unprepared."

"I am going to die, Dr. Parker. I will die at some point. And whether it's now or years from now, whatever is on the other side will still be there."

"Very true, Carol. Now, if there is a God waiting for you, what would you say to him?"

"I made a lot of mistakes, but I did the best I could." Carol said with conviction.

"Very good, Carol. I am impressed. This is a very bold

step for you. I am really proud of you."

"Thanks." Carol smiled. She had genuine peace in her heart and Dr. Parker could see it in her eyes.

Chapter 16

Dear Alex, Remember how you told me that you were relieved when your mom died? How her suffering was over and all of that? I know that nobody knows what happens after we die, and I'm okay with that. I really hope you're right. I hope your mom isn't suffering any more. I hope you're not suffering any more. I hope that I won't suffer for too much longer. I want you and your mom and my dad and everyone else to be out of pain.

More than anything, I hope I see you again. I miss you so much, Alex. You are my everything. I love you so much, Alexandria Whetherby. I am not complete without you. You are my love and my life. I don't know if this really has any point or not. I just want you to know that I really hope you're right. I love you. I miss you. Hopefully I'll see you soon.

Shelby walked in just as Carol changed channels and an old musical came on the TV.

"A musical?" Shelby brightly asked.

"Yeah. I do kind of like the old musicals. They were fun and innocent. I'd like to see those musicals made for the gay community, like, Lesbianism: The Musical, Or Seven Brides for Seven Sisters, or even Okla-Homosexual."

Shelby burst out into laughter. "Oh dear God. That's terrible, Carol." She sputtered between chuckles.

"I can say it, I'm a lesbian. Seriously, it would be nice to have those same sweet romantic stories about us."

Shelby quieted her laughter. "I can understand that. I just don't see you as a musical person. I always pictured you watching war movies."

"I did. My father and I used to watch all kinds of war and historical movies all the time. I do love war movies and the memories of spending time with my dad." Carol paused wistfully. "When I was thirteen or fourteen, I wrote an essay in school about all the various roles women had in the civil war. The essay actually won a prize."

"Oh wow, good for you. I bet your dad was really proud of you."

"Yeah, he was." Carol replied softly. "After that, any time we'd watch a civil war movie, I'd always point out the soldiers that I thought were women disguised as men so they could fight." She shrugged. "Of course I realized when I was older that I was just pointing at actors."

Shelby chuckled. "That's funny."

"Yeah. We kind of made a game of it. We had a lot of fun. We always enjoyed the war movies anyway, but that was an added bonus that just he and I shared."

"That's really sweet, Carol. Those sound like some great memories."

"They are," Carol smiled.

"You need to cherish those." Shelby said.

"I do." Carol replied.

"Sometimes I just wish I could reach out and hold her hand again." Carol said.

"You can hold her twin's hand," Byron replied. Byron took off his glove so Carol could hold his hand.

Carol looked up at Byron with a docile and fragile look in

her eyes. She hesitated to touch him. Byron gently placed Carol's small, IV-ridden hand into his own large, warm hand.

Carol remained silent for several minutes. "Your sister was my first, Byron."

"I thought you had dated other women before her." Byron said confused.

"I had. I dated a couple of girls in high school, but never anything serious."

"Why not? You're a sweet girl. You didn't have a classic intense high school romance?"

"No, not at all." Carol looked down at the floor. "I was more of a science experiment."

"Huh?" Byron was puzzled.

Slowly, Carol raised her head to look him in the eyes. "Those girls weren't like me, B. They were just curious or wanted to toy with my emotions by dating me and then spreading horrible rumors about me through the school. I was just an experiment or a joke to them. Nothing more." She grimaced at the memory. "I've always been a shy person. I didn't date at all in college. Not until I met Alex. I was too afraid. But the minute I saw Alex, I knew she was different. I just knew that I could trust her and my heart would be safe."

"That makes everything that much more special," Byron replied gently.

"Yeah."

"You know that you were the best thing to ever happen to Alex?" Byron paused. "She was just a little older than you, but she had several bad relationships. All the people Alex encountered were users. They used her to get drunk or high or for whatever they could imagine. You know how generous she was. She'd give them whatever they wanted and they took full advantage of that. They enabled her drinking, big time. She went through the ringer more than once."

Carol could see that Byron was smiling.

"Then she met you. She called me all excited and told me about you the day after you two met. She instantly knew there was something different about you. She knew you weren't like the others she had dated. She knew she found someone special. It was funny how she rambled on and on about you."

Carol smiled brightly, thinking of Alex being so happy and excited after their first meeting so many years before.

"When she wanted you to come over on Valentine's Day, she called me up begging me to let her have wine with you." Byron continued. "I brought over the wine and she was so excited about having you over. She wouldn't shut up about you! I just wanted to drop it off and go, but she kept talking about you and her plans for the night. She was like a little kid on Christmas. I was skeptical, but I really hoped that you would be different; that you wouldn't use her like the others had."

"When I came back the day after, to get the rest of the wine and help her clean up, she was so happy. I had never seen her so happy in my life." Byron paused and saw tears forming in Carol's eyes. "She loved you immediately, Carol. She told me you were unlike any other person.

"When you moved in she was so excited. I'll admit, I was nervous. She had people move in before and it never turned out well. I was afraid that you'd throw her sobriety right out the window. But you didn't. I've never seen you drink. You don't drink much, do you? Were you always like that or did you do that for her?"

"I don't know. I never really thought about it, Byron. I just knew that she was clean and I never wanted to tempt her. It would have been extremely selfish of me to drink in front of her. On the rare occasion I did want to, I'd ask her first to make sure she was okay with it. Truth be told, I could live without it. So, it worked out well for both of us."

Byron smiled down at Carol. "She always said you were

different. You know what? She was right. She was absolutely right. You were different from all those losers. You encouraged her to stay sober. You gave to her, you never took from her. You supported her. You were really good to her. You treated her like a queen, Carol." Byron smiled.

"That's because she was a queen, Byron. She was my queen."

Byron gently wrapped his warm hand around Carol's. Using what little strength she had, Carol squeezed Byron's fingers.

"When it's right, it's right." Byron said with a tranquil smile.

Carol was silent for several moments. "But, we fought, Byron. It was never perfect."

Byron laughed. "Of course you fought, Carol. People always fight. Put any two people in a room together, they are bound to fight sooner or later. Nothing is ever perfect, but what you two had was damn close, the closest I've ever seen. We all could take a cue from you two. Seriously, you and Alex had the best relationship I have ever seen."

Carol lips slowly curled into a smile. Byron smiled back.

"Thanks," Carol whispered.

"No, thank you, Carol. Thank you for all that you did for Alex. You were the best thing to ever happen to her. Don't ever let anyone tell you otherwise."

"Okay," Carol choked before tears began escaping her brown eyes.

Shelby turned the light on in Carol's room as she entered. The early winter darkness had cast the room into a vast, black space. Carol winced at the bright light.

"Oh, I'm sorry. Did I wake you, Carol?" Shelby asked softly.

“No, no.” Carol stretched her arms as best she could.

“I didn’t mean to disturb you.”

“It’s fine, Shelby.” Carol paused to think about her daily life in this hospital. “Hey Shelby, when will all of this be over?” Carol asked innocently.

“It’ll all be over when you’re ready, Carol. When you’re all better.” Shelby replied with what Carol assumed was a small smile under her mask. Shelby looked at Carol’s chart. “I need to get something. I’ll be right back,” Shelby said as she turned to leave the room.

Just as she did, Byron entered. “Hi Shelby.”

“Hi Byron,” Shelby replied brightly.

“Shelby,” Byron gently pulled Shelby aside. He whispered, “let me ask you a question. Is Carol eating okay?” There was concern in his tone.

“Yes, Carol’s eating well. Why?”

“Look at her. She’s always been thin, but now, now she’s emaciated. She’s lost so much weight.” Byron was distressed.

“I know. I can see you’re concerned. In her case, there are a lot of factors to consider. Unfortunately, this kind of weight loss is not uncommon with HIV/AIDS patients, Byron. But, she *is* eating well and doing well over-all.”

“That’s good to hear. Thanks.” Byron smiled at Shelby. He was only slightly reassured. He went to Carol’s bed as Shelby left the room. “Hey.”

“Heya, B. How are you?” Carol tried to sit up higher in her bed.

“Same old, same old. How are you?”

“Ditto”

“Yeah, well...” Byron started to speak as Tyrone walked into the room.

“Oh hey, Tyrone,” Carol greeted him brightly.

“Hi Carol,” Tyrone replied. “How are you doing today?”

“Same medical bullshit, different day.” Carol paused for a minute. “Are Erin and Candace on their way up?”

“No,” Byron answered after a brief pause. “Just us boys today. Hope that’s okay.”

“Ah, the boys. Of course it’s okay.” Carol said. “You know, I always wanted to be one of the boys.”

The three remained in an awkward silence for several moments.

“You are, in your own right.” Tyrone said, smiling weakly.

“I wish.” Carol retorted. “If I was a guy, people wouldn’t have hated me so much. Instead I’m considered weird because I’m a woman who loved another woman. People just love hating gay folks. You guys are really lucky.”

“I suppose so,” Byron replied. “But remember, you are still talking to two black men. It hasn’t always been an easy ride for us either, Carol.”

Carol sighed. Why was it that the three of them had experienced prejudice of any sort? “I suppose it hasn’t been. Why do people have to hate other people because of the color of their skin or the person they love? Why are people so full of hate?” Carol’s eyes danced between the two men hoping for an answer and some solace.

“I don’t know, Carol.” Tyrone finally answered.

“Fear. Ignorance.” Byron ticked off answers.

“But that doesn’t justify their words or actions.” Carol protested with as much strength as she had.

“No it doesn’t. You’re right. The truth is, nothing does. That kind of behavior is not justifiable. Not in any way.” Tyrone responded.

Carol took in a deep breath. “I just wish it didn’t have to be this way.” She said softly.

“Agreed,” Byron replied. “Trust me. We hate it as much as you do, Carol. It’s not right. There’s no reason for such hatred.”

“I just wish…” Carol started.

Shelby came back into Carol’s room. “Alright, Miss Carol, time for a new PCA. This new medication may make you a bit sleepy.”

“Okay, we’ll get out of here.” Byron said quickly. He turned to Tyrone. “Let’s go home.”

“Home? Please, please let me go home too,” Carol pleaded.

“Soon, Carol. You’ll be coming home with us soon enough.” Byron replied as he tenderly squeezed her small hand. He and Tyrone wished Carol and Shelby a good night before they left Carol’s isolated hospital room.

“I just want to get out of here. I envy that you guys get to go home,” Carol whined to Candace.

“I know, sweetie. Soon. You’ll be able to leave here soon.” Candace gently rubbed Carol’s arm. “And when you are, we’ll all be there celebrating with you and spending time with you at home.”

“But you’ll have to go back to your own homes eventually. And I’ll be forced to live alone. To live a life without Alex.”

“Carol, what do you know about monarch butterflies?” Candace asked without missing a beat.

“Nothing. Why?”

“Let me tell you about them. Monarch caterpillars eat

until right before they cocoon. Then, they form their little cocoon. While they're in there, they eat themselves to near death."

"Really?" Carol asked, horrified.

"It's true. They leave just a few cells remaining to regenerate and create the butterfly. This takes ten days to two weeks, which for a butterfly is more than a lifetime." Candace stopped to take a breath. "Once they're re-born, they come out of the cocoon and they need to re-learn how to walk and learn how to fly. They stretch their wings using new muscles and walk around re-learning how to coordinate their little legs. Once they're strong and sure of themselves, they fly away to go live a new life as a butterfly."

"So, you're telling me that when I come out of this cocoon of a hospital, I'll be a beautiful butterfly and fly away. Thanks, but I don't do clichés, Candace."

"No, no. That's not what I'm saying, Carol. What I'm saying is that you need to re-learn how to walk. You need to learn how to coordinate your life again. You need to learn how to use new muscles you never had before. These are the muscles of a life without Alex. If a butterfly can do it, you can certainly learn how to live life as a new creature."

"But I don't want to be a new creature."

"You don't have a choice, sweetie. It just is. Just like the caterpillars. They have no choice. They have to transform into a butterfly. That's just the way it is."

Carol sulked. "How do you know all this any way?"

"A few years back, Byron took out his air compressor for a job he was doing and there was a little caterpillar hanging upside down on it. The next day, it was in its cocoon. Byron was really concerned about the little guy. I started doing research on caterpillars and butterflies for him. He used his air compressor for his nail gun and big paint jobs. That's powerful stuff. Definitely not safe for a tiny little caterpillar."

She paused and her shoulders shook as she laughed quietly. "Byron needed to use the air compressor, so he did, just very carefully. He eventually named the caterpillar John Wayne because it was such a tough little bug hanging on to this big construction air compressor. Day in and day out, Byron worked and used the air compressor, but he always made sure he checked on John Wayne throughout the day."

Carol chuckled at the butterfly's name.

"It was about two weeks later that the little guy hatched and we got to watch him fly away. It was really amazing."

"I'll bet."

"Now if a tiny insect can hang on to a large, loud, vibrating construction grade air compressor and re-learn how to walk and fly, you can definitely re-learn how to live as a new creature. A new Carol."

Carol was silent. Her eyes turned to the floor. It was obvious that the thought of a life without Alex was repulsive to her.

"Go on and be cynical if you want to, Carol, but I have faith in you."

Carol sighed. "Thanks, C." She sounded dejected. "I appreciate it. You've been a good source of comfort for me through all this."

Candace smiled warmly. "Carol, do you remember the night you and Alex told us you had AIDS? Byron flipped out and Alex went over to talk to him while you apologized to me and comforted me. Do you remember that?"

Carol hesitated. "Yeah."

"I remember it vividly. It's something I've never forgotten. It meant a lot to me then and it still does now. Now, it's my time to comfort and apologize to you.

"I'm sorry that Byron and I were rude to you when we first met you. I'm sorry we had all the problems that we had.

I'm sorry that Byron was able to get married and I got pregnant and you and Alex couldn't do any of that. I'm sorry."

"It's okay, Candace. You have no control over gay marriage or our being able to start a family."

"Just like you had no control over getting AIDS from a blood transfusion more than twenty years ago. Got it?"

Carol smiled tentatively. "Yeah. Thanks."

"You're welcome, sweetie. It's getting late. I need to get home to Tyrone." Candace lifted her pregnant body out of the chair and slowly walked towards the door.

Carol hesitated before calling out. "Hey Candace? Is Tyrone good to you?"

Candace stopped and turned back to Carol. "What?"

"Is Tyrone good to you? He seems like a good guy when he's around us. I just want to know he really is like that."

"He's no different from what you've seen. He's excellent. He's a good man, Carol. I am extremely blessed to have him."

"Then why don't you two get married?"

Candace laughed heartily. "I've been waiting for someone to ask me that. I thought it would be Byron, not you. Tyrone has proposed, but I said no."

Carol was stunned. "Why not?"

"He asked me when we first found out I was pregnant. I told him I love him and I am committed to him, but I don't want to get married until my older sister and her partner of twelve years can get married. It's only fair."

Carol was surprised. Her wide eyes tried to absorb the smile, and the wisdom, in Candace's face. "Wow. Candace... thank you. That's, that's incredible."

Candace smiled down at Carol. "I may not be homosexual or bisexual. That doesn't mean your equal rights aren't just as important to me."

Carol stared back at Candace. “Thank you. That’s all I can say. Thank you so much, Candace.”

“You’re welcome sweetie. Now, you get some good rest and I’ll see you tomorrow.”

“Okay. Good night.” Carol was smiling as she watched Candace slowly waddle out of the room.

Chapter 17

A cold, hard winter rain pelted Carol's window. The rain smacking against the building sounded reminded Carol of popcorn popping. Carol sighed, wishing she could feel the rain hit her skin.

"Hi Carol," Shelby said as she came into the room. "Time for us to check your values again."

"Alright," Carol mumbled.

Shelby began organizing all of her necessary blood tubes, syringes and labels.

"Shelby?" Carol interrupted her.

"Yes, Carol?"

"What's it like outside?" There was a child-like innocence to Carol's voice.

"Cold and rainy." Shelby dismissed the question and the weather.

"No, tell me what it's really like. What it looks like, what it smells like, what it feels like." Carol paused briefly. "Does it smell like rain?"

Shelby hesitated. "No. I'm sorry, Carol. The rain is so cold and so hard you can't really smell anything. It doesn't have that sweet rain smell like it does in the spring."

"Okay. What does everything look like? Is it pretty outside or...?"

"Well, the trees are pretty ugly and bare. There's ice on them, though, so they kind of twinkle in the light." Shelby feigned a weak smile. "There are a few patches of green peeking through the snow."

Carol immediately perked up. "What shade of green?"

Shelby thought for a moment. "Light green. Baby grass green. And the snow is dull and greyish. That's not pretty at all."

"Oh that's too bad," Carol mumbled. "What is the wind like, Shelby?"

"Oh, ick. It's nasty. It's pretty strong. It's one of those cold, bone-chilling, winter-y winds. You know, typical disgusting winter weather."

Carol paused and looked down at her IV-ridden hand. She studied her pale, wrinkled, and bruised skin. "Shelby, can you do me a favor?"

"Yeah, Carol. What's up?"

"Could you stop and just enjoy the weather for me for a minute the next time you're out? Look at the grass and snow. Take in a deep breath of fresh air. Feel the rain hitting your skin. Just think of me. I'd really like to experience all of that again. But if you could do it for me?"

Shelby paused for a moment, thinking how much of daily life she took for granted. "Yeah, Carol. I will." She replied softly.

Dear Alex, How are we supposed to go on when the most important person in our lives is gone? Without you, I have no life; no purpose. What is the sense in me carrying on when I have nothing left? I can't watch a baseball game without thinking about you. I have no reason to work or do anything, I did it all for you. Without you, there is no reason for me to do anything. Life has no purpose if you're not here. What's the point?

It just seems to me that if you have lost your purpose in

life, there's no reason to keep living. There's nothing left. I just can't imagine any kind of life for myself without you. I don't think I can go on if you're not with me. I'm actually not depressed, baby. It's just that you're just too damn important to me.

Carol paused to think of the words she had just written and the words that still had to be written.

I guess that's it for now. I love you, sweetheart. And I always will.

Carol closed the journal and closed her eyes, picturing Alex's beautiful face wearing a warm, bright smile. Alex's perfect, white teeth and wide grin was captivating, even when simply imagined. Imagining Alex's smile caused Carol to wear a small smile of her own as she gradually drifted off to sleep.

Carol quietly watched the sun set on yet another day outside her hospital room window.

Watching the sun slowly slip behind the buildings brought her peace even in the confines of her sterile hospital room. Carol felt calm and serene despite her surroundings.

Carol was mesmerized by the bright colors that painted the sky. The sun was a blindingly bright orange hue. The sky embracing the orange orb was a pristine pastel pink. Just above the pink clouds was a vibrant violet color. The purple faded upwards into a beautiful brilliant blue. The encroaching night sky rested above it all.

Carol breathed deeply trying to inhale the colors.

The sunset and this moment was truly impeccable.

Shelby entered Carol's room. "Is there anything you need

before I leave for the night?" She asked.

"Yeah," Carol's voice creaked. "Shelby, remember how you told me you wouldn't forget me? You told me that your patients impacted you as much as you did them."

"Yes, that's true. Why?" Shelby sounded confused.

"Who are they?"

Shelby simply looked at Carol.

"Who are they, Shelby? Tell me about the patients that had an impact on you."

"Well... there was Mrs. Crabtree."

"Who was she?" Carol asked.

"Mrs. Crabtree was an elderly lady. She was here for about three months, I think.

"Every day she would tell me stories of her life: all the places she had seen; funny stories of her kids growing up; interesting and even bizarre life stories that often seemed made up, but she swore they were true." Shelby lightly chuckled.

Carol smiled, trying to imagine what stories this old woman had conjured up. "What about her affected you most?"

Shelby stopped to think for a moment. "She was so satisfied with her life. She always wanted to travel more, but she was very content with the experiences she already had. She really taught me how to appreciate everything I have."

Carol was listening intently.

"She passed away here in the hospital. Right before she died, she smiled at me and told me to remember all of her stories. I promised her I would. Some of the details are fuzzy, but I remember them for the most part. Moreover, I remember her."

"Who else?" Carol asked without hesitation.

Shelby took a deep breath. "I'll never forget Mr. Hamilton."

"Why?"

"He had no family. His parents died young and he was an only child. He had been in one of the worst car accidents I had ever seen. He was with us for long time. But you know what the kicker was? He was always really cheerful. I'm sure he felt lonely, but he never let on. He was chipper every morning. I don't remember hearing him complain once. He just focused on getting better every day." Shelby nodded as she remembered him. "When he left here, he had a new job waiting for him. He was so excited to go out and date again, too. He had a lot of gusto and enthusiasm. He just loved being alive. He had a great smile, too. His positive attitude was really contagious."

Carol was silent for a moment. "Are there more?"

"Oh, sure," Shelby answered brightly. "There was Elaine. She was a little girl and she was mauled by a dog."

"Oh my God," Carol whispered.

"She was one brave little girl. She let us do anything and everything we needed to. She didn't whine or complain ever. She cried a few times, but she was amazingly stoic for a little girl. And you know what? She didn't care if her face was scarred or disfigured. When she left here, she was just happy to be with her family. The scars meant nothing. We could all learn a lesson in humility from her."

"Yeah," Carol whispered.

"Mr. Riviera was a poor soul who was dying from Chondrosarcoma, a type of bone cancer. It was awful, he really suffered. He was in tremendous pain all the time. He was really brave, though. He wasn't afraid to die. He was at peace with everything. When he finally passed, it was actually quite a relief. He wasn't in any more pain. I miss him, but I'm glad his suffering is over."

Carol hardly waited before she spoke up. "Those were all regular ICU cases. Have you ever had any other isolation cases like me?"

"Yes, of course. We see it all, Carol. But if I told you about all the patients I've had over the years, we'd be here forever."

Carol quietly sighed. "I guess so."

"Does that help?" Shelby asked.

"I think so," Carol lied. She wondered about all the other patients who supposedly touched Shelby, yet she didn't discuss them? Why not? Would Carol end up being grouped together with this anonymous bunch that wasn't worth mentioning?

"Alright then. Good night, Carol."

"Good night, Shelby." Carol turned to look out the window so Shelby couldn't see her tears.

Dear Alex, I miss you. Damn. I miss you so much. It's so hard not being with you. Remember that silly Valentine poem I wrote to you a few years back? Roses are red, violets blue. I am gay and so are you.

Carol laughed out loud as she scribbled out the words.

I hope so. That was fun. I love those funny memories. Do you remember all the times we'd just look at each other and say 'inconceivable' like that guy in The Princess Bride? We were always so silly with each other. I loved that about us. We didn't take things too seriously. You had the most beautiful, addicting laugh I have ever heard. I'd do anything to hear that laugh again. Remember going to the gay book store with Dave and John?

Carol sighed as she recalled all of her sweet memories with Alexandria. Carol's vision became slightly blurry as tiny tears began to form.

Do you remember I told you how wonderful you are? You really are. I hope I told you that enough. Remember me telling you how pretty you are? You are, Alex. You're the most beautiful woman in the world. In ancient Egypt, Nefertiti was supposedly the most beautiful woman to ever walk the Earth. Her name even means 'the beautiful one has arrived.' But they were wrong. She had nothing on you, babe. You are, by far, the most beautiful woman there ever was. I hope I told you that enough too.

All those times I told you I loved you, I meant it. I still do. Love doesn't even describe how I feel. I adore you. I love you with every inch of my being. The words 'I love you' are weak compared to how I feel about you. I hope I told you I love you enough. I never want you to doubt it. Not even for one millisecond. I often wonder if I said or did things enough. Enough for you to really feel it, to know it. I guess I'll never really know. But it is all true. I mean all of it, Alex. Eternity isn't enough time for me to tell you and to be sure that it is enough. I love you.

Carol closed her journal before her tears overwhelmed her.

Byron looked anxiously at the clock in Carol's room. "She should be here by now."

"Something must have taken longer than expected. I'm sure she'll be back soon." Candace said, trying to calm the group.

"I don't know. We're never this late in the home," Erin said pessimistically.

Everyone stood in Carol's room in silence. After several moments, the door opened and Shelby jogged in.

"I am so sorry I'm late with your evening meds, Carol. I just got so tied up. We had a guest musician here today, and..."

“Really?” Carol’s face lit up with the excitement of a change from her usual routine and visitors.

“Yeah. She’s been here all day. It’s been hard to keep all the meds on track while she’s been wandering around.”

“When is she coming here?” Carol asked excitedly.

Shelby paused for a moment. “Oh she’s not coming in here, Carol. I am so sorry.” She injected several different syringes into Carol’s IV lines.

Carol’s face dropped. Her disappointment was obvious. Carol looked away sadly.

“That’s too bad,” Erin snapped.

“Yeah,” Shelby mumbled, her face focused on Carol’s various IVs. Shelby stood up after a moment. Byron touched her arm and motioned her away from the group.

“Shelby, why can’t she come in here and sing to Carol. Do you see how disappointed she is? What harm can it do for this woman to spend just five minutes singing to her?”

“Mr. Whetherby, I wish she could. I’m sorry. She just can’t come in here. She’s been all over the hospital. Who knows what germs she might have picked up? It’s just too much of a risk for Carol.”

Byron grunted. “We suit up every time we’re in here, wear masks and gloves to protect her. Why can’t she do the same?”

“We can’t guard a guitar against germs and I’m sure it would be difficult for her to play with gloves on. I’m sorry, I really am. There’s nothing I can do about it.”

“Fine,” Byron was annoyed. “Carol, are you going to be okay for the evening?” He asked.

“Yeah,” Carol muttered back.

“Try to get some good rest.” Erin said, touching Carol’s arm. “We’ll all be back tomorrow to visit with you.”

"Honey, we love you." Candace slowly rose to her feet.

"Love you too," Carol said listlessly.

Everyone wished Carol a good night and Shelby followed them out of the room. Carol was alone, again.

"Hey," Carol squealed.

"Hi" Will and Robyn said in unison.

"What's up?"

"Just took a breather from work, figured we'd come up and see you." Will answered.

Carol looked up at Robyn. She was as beautiful as ever. Her eyes twinkled in the light, and she gently smiled at Carol. "How are you, Carol?" Robyn asked gently.

"Okay, I guess. Nothing ever changes here, Robyn."

"That painting changed," Robyn pointed out the artwork on the wall.

"Oh yeah, that. That was my 'art therapy' a little while back. I don't know how long ago I actually painted it. Every day just blurs into the next. It's basically one, terrible, unending day here."

"I'm so sorry." Robyn answered.

"How's my Sug-sug?" Carol asked, trying to think of happier subjects.

Will hesitated.

"Good. Everything is good." Robyn jumped in.

"That's good. I miss her, you know."

"We know," Will said.

"What's going on at Dawson?"

"Not much. Nate's been working like a fiend. He's a hard

worker. No more ordering problems or unhappy customers like we had when..."

"Good," Carol cut him off. "That's good to hear."

"A lot of the clients have been asking about you." Will said, changing his tone.

"Yeah? What have you told them?"

"Just that were looking forward to you coming back soon." Will smiled.

Carol chuckled. "Thanks, Will." Carol turned her attention back to Robyn.

"How's school been going?"

"Good. I have pretty good students this year. One was just diagnosed with a learning disability, but he seems to be doing well in my class. Just a few minutes of extra time and he's fine."

"That's so nice that you do that for him."

"I have to. It's my job." Robyn laughed a bright and cheerful laugh.

"Well, I still think it's great. The world needs more teachers like you," Carol softly said.

"Thank you, Carol."

Will looked at his watch. "Well, visiting hours are almost over and..."

Carol felt the loss begin to set in. Will seemed uncomfortable around her. He'd leave as soon as he came each time he visited. "You just got here, Will."

"I know. I'm sorry it's a short visit."

"Every visit has been a short visit. Why don't you ever stay?"

Will and Robyn looked at each other.

"Well, you see, Carol..." Robyn started.

Will took a deep breath. "I can't stand seeing you like this."

"I don't like being here like this, either, but I'm forced to. I don't have a choice. I thought we were friends, Will."

"We are, Carol." He pleaded. "It's just, you shouldn't be here. You shouldn't be cooped up, hooked up to all kinds of IVs and machines."

Carol took a deep breath. "I'm sorry, Will. I really am. I don't want to be here, either. I fucking hate it here. I'm all alone. If someone wants to visit me, they have to dress like it's a nuclear war. All they do is suck my blood and fill my veins back up with all kinds of shit. I hate it. But I don't get the luxury of going home whenever I want to."

Will looked at the ground. "I'm so sorry," he said quietly. "I never meant to hurt you. I guess it's easy to forget what you're going through while we're at home. I'm sorry, Carol."

Carol sighed. "It's okay, Will. I love you both. I just wish I could spend some real time with my friends."

Will and Robyn both nodded.

Carol forced a smile. "You two get home before it gets too late. Just don't forget about me, okay?"

"Never," Robyn promised.

"We won't," Will replied.

"Good night," Robyn said as they walked out the door.

Dave and John crept into Carol's room almost as if they were in some spy movie. Carol could see that under Dave's bunny suit he wore a sharp dress suit. He carried his briefcase with him.

"Are they looking?" He asked anxiously.

John looked around. "I don't think so."

"Good," Dave whispered.

"Guys, what's going on?" Carol was amused.

"We've been worried that all you've been eating is hospital food. And, well..." John started.

"You're too damn thin, girl!" Dave exclaimed.

Carol laughed.

"We snuck some food in for you," John said covertly.

"From La Cucina. We know how much you love their food." Dave murmured.

Carol's eyes lit up. "La Cucina? I haven't had that in ages. Wow, thank you so much." Carol's voice seemed to echo loudly in her room.

"Sssssh." Dave said with a finger over his mouth. "Here," he opened his brief case. Inside was a large, round container with steam rolling off it, and the incredible, enticing smell of well-cooked pasta.

"It's just pasta primavera. I hope that's okay," John said, handing Carol a plastic fork.

"Oh, it's perfect. Thank you so much." Carol quickly began shoveling the noodles and vegetables into her mouth.

"I guess she likes it," John joked with Dave.

Dave shot John a serious look. "I'm going to keep an eye out. I don't want anyone catching her and taking it away." He sounded nervous.

"Relax," John gently advised him. "I'm sure it'll be fine. We came in late enough."

Carol continued to savor every sweet, spicy, juicy bite of her pasta dinner.

"How have you been, Carol?" John asked.

Carol looked up at him with a mouth full of food. "Good," she garbled.

John laughed. "Good. I'm glad to see you're hanging in there. You are one tough cookie. We're really proud of you."

"Thanks," Carol said as she swallowed her food. "What ever happened with that grocery job?"

"I got it," John answered. "It's not glamorous by any means. But it's a steady pay check."

"It's such a shame, John. You're a professional and you're extremely creative. You should be working at the ad agency."

"I know. But times are tough. I'm lucky I got this job. We know quite a few people who were laid off a year ago or more and they still haven't found jobs."

"Wow, that's scary. I didn't realize just how bad it really is," Carol said.

"Well, you know how it goes. It takes time to rebuild after something like that. Everyone would like an instant cure, but it's just not going to happen," John said wisely. "I'm sure that once things pick back up, I can get to working at the agency again or with another one. I'm not worried about it."

"I'm worried about Nurse Helga," Dave said coming back to Carol's bedside. "Hurry, so you don't get in trouble."

Carol laughed. "You are too paranoid, Dave."

"I just don't want you to be stuck with just the slop they serve here."

"I appreciate it," Carol said with a smile before she took in another fork-full of delicious pasta.

"Everyone at the office sends their love." Dave said.

"Oh, that's sweet. Give them all my regards," Carol replied.

"Oh, I will," Dave answered with a huge grin on his face.

Carol scraped every last morsel from the container. "That was great. Thank you both so much."

"It's good to see you with your belly full." John smiled.

"Indeed," Dave agreed.

"This really means the world to me. You're great friends. Thank you." Carol said. Dave and John could see tears forming in Carol's eyes.

"You're welcome," John replied softly.

"Let me take this," Dave said softly as he hid the dish and fork back in his brief case. "Now, you be good. Okay, Missy?"

"I will. You guys have to go already?" Carol asked. She felt the inevitable sadness creeping in.

"I'm sorry. One of the nurses told us we only had fifteen minutes." Dave responded.

"Oh," Carol said dismally. "Okay. Will I see you guys soon?"

"You bet," Dave assured her.

"Take good care, Carol." John said, smiling at her again.

"You two, too." She smiled back.

"Bye," Dave said as the pair walked out.

Carol sighed and closed her eyes. It was easy to feel sleepy after eating a full meal. She enjoyed it so much. She allowed her mind to drift and thought about more food from La Cucina.

Dear Alex, You'll never believe what happened to me today. There was a guest musician at the hospital recently. She sang for almost every patient in the hospital. Every patient but me. They told me she wasn't allowed to come in and sing for me because it would be too much of a risk for my health. I think that's a crock. Everyone was here when it happened, but we all just dismissed it. I never really gave it a second thought. Tyrone and Candace came to visit today. It wasn't just a regular visit.

They came in and Tyrone was carrying a big guitar case. He told me they made him disinfect it like crazy. It's amazing they even let him bring it in. Tyrone took out his guitar and Candace sang. They played a bunch of songs for me, Alex. It was great! They played Hendrix's Angel. That was amazing. Hearing Candace singing those lyrics only made me think of you. It was absolutely beautiful. I wish you could have heard it, babe. You would have loved it, too.

Then they sang Pink Floyd's Wish You Were Here. I never imagined I'd ever hear Candace sing a song like that. She did really well. She told me that they couldn't decide between that, Mother, Another Brick in the Wall and a few others. I was floored. I'm starting to wonder if your little sister digs Pink Floyd as much as we do. It certainly seems that way. Anyway, they did a really good job of it. Tyrone's guitar playing is just incredible and Candace sang Floyd as well as anyone else I've ever heard.

They also played Going to California by Led Zep. That was so beautiful. Tyrone strummed his guitar like a professional. Hearing Candace sing that slow, pretty song was perfect. It really suited her nice voice. That one really touched me, Alex.

They sang three The Who songs. That was cool. They sang Happy Jack, which I haven't heard in ages. They harmonized throughout the whole thing. They did a fun rendition. They also sang Pinball Wizard, you have to if you're going to sing The Who. I almost thought Tyrone was going to break a string the way he was playing his guitar for that one. Last they sang Who Are You. That was fun too. I think that's another obligatory The Who song. It was fun. I sang along with them doing the "who who who" part in the chorus. I'm sure I sounded terrible, but it was still fun.

Tyrone plays well, very well. That kid is really talented, babe. Candace has a beautiful voice. Not as beautiful as yours, but still pretty. They told me they picked those songs because they knew how much we loved classic rock. Even though it wasn't their type of music, they learned and practiced all those songs for me. Can you believe it? They did something just extraordinary for me, Alex. It was the nicest, sweetest thing. I'm still in shock that they would do something like that, it was so good. It was incredible, babe. It really was.

You have a great family, my love. I am so lucky to have them all as my in-laws. They're really good people. Thank you, sweetheart. Thank you for being the best thing that ever happened to me. Thank you for introducing me to such a great family. I don't know where I'd be without the Whetherby's.

Carol sighed thinking about Alex and her family. She picked the pen up again and continued writing.

I love you so much, baby. I miss you like hell. I wish you were here. Maybe someday soon I'll be in your arms again. I love you, baby.

Carol gently closed the book and let her tears fall before she finally found sleep.

The people in the room couldn't avoid listening in to the argument in the hallway.

"Look, I don't care what you say. This is my baby and my family. You can't stop me from doing what I want." Candace's voice echoed through the hospital hallway. "That's fine. I've taken your advisory into consideration, but I am still seeing my sister-in-law." Candace paused for a few moments. "My condition is my concern, not yours."

Candace came into Carol's room mumbling under her

breath. "Tell me I can't see my own family. Condition. I don't have a condition. I'm pregnant and I will do as I damn well please. Nurse freakin' Betty."

Candace slowly trudged through the room and finally made her way to Carol. "Hey, sweetie girl." She tried to sound very positive.

"Hey," Carol replied, a look of concern and confusion on her face. "You okay?"

"Oh yeah. Just some stupid nurse telling me I can't see you because I'm pregnant."

Everyone in the room remained silent as they looked at one another.

"Baby, maybe you ought..." Tyrone spoke up.

"Ought to what? Listen to that ignorance? If I did everything they told me to do, I'd have been stuck in bed in a dark room without contact with any of you months ago. It's all just plain stupid." Candace replied. She turned back to Carol. "Anyway, how are you, Carol?"

Carol chuckled. "Good, Candace. I'm good. Nothing new really going on here. Nothing's ever going on here, really. I wonder if anything ever will happen."

The door to Carol's room suddenly opened with a loud thud. "I have an announcement for all of you." Dr. Ramone spoke as he entered Carol's room.

Tyrone, Candace, Byron and Erin all stood around Carol's bed waiting for the doctor's next words.

"We finally have some good news," Dr. Ramone exclaimed. Everyone's face, even Carol's, lit up in anticipation.

"Our patient will have her first surgery next week."

Everyone breathed a sigh of relief and smiled.

"Finally," Carol mumbled.

"What are you doing first?" Byron asked cautiously.

"The pelvic injuries have potentially life-threatening consequences, so that is what we will tend to first." Dr. Ramone explained matter-of-factly.

"How long will the surgery last?" Candace sounded concerned.

"That's really hard to tell, Ms. Whetherby. Even under normal circumstances, this isn't a quick procedure. Dr. J and I have consulted with the top orthopedic surgeon here, and we're all on the same page.

"Surgery won't be quick or easy, but Carol is in excellent hands."

Candace snorted quietly.

"What do we do between now and then?" Tyrone asked.

"Carol needs plenty of rest, support and encouragement. Support each other as well, it'll make a world of difference." He smiled reassuringly at the group. "Are there any other questions?"

They looked from one to another in silence.

"No. Thank you, doctor." Erin spoke quietly.

"You're welcome."

"Carol, I'll be in later to discuss all of the treatment details with you."

"Okay," Carol quietly responded.

Dr. Ramone nodded to everyone in the room before he walked out.

There was an awkward, tense in the room for several minutes after Dr. Ramone exited.

"Are you ready for this?" Byron softly asked Carol.

She looked up at him. "I have to be," she said stoically.

Chapter 18

Byron walked hesitantly into Carol's room. The setting winter sun left tiny pools of light on the floor. "Hey," his deep voice cracked as he spoke.

"Hey Byron," Carol replied weakly. It seemed a strain for her to speak.

"Oh dear God," Byron whispered.

"What?" Carol squeaked.

"It's worse than I thought."

"What is?"

"You've been getting weaker, not stronger. You're about to go into surgery, but you can't. Not like this." Byron broke down and cried.

Carol took in a deep breath and slowly exhaled. "Byron, what is going on?"

Byron wept.

Carol sighed heavily. "B, I'm prepared for whatever happens. They think I can handle this surgery. I'm sure it'll be fine."

"No it won't. Dear God, it won't. Please Carol, don't do this."

"Don't do what, Byron?"

"Don't have the surgery. Don't die. I can't lose you too."

Carol looked at Byron. What had brought this large, strong man to his knees? "I don't understand," Carol whispered.

"Carol, I've been wrong all along. I've been wrong since the day I met you. I was so wrong about you." He sniffled. "Alex is gone. I lost my twin and you are the closest thing I have to her now. I can't lose you too. You mean so much to me."

"Thank you, Byron," Carol said softly.

Byron continued, "Carol, I was wrong to judge you because you're white. I was wrong to judge you because you're gay. I was wrong to hate you because you're HIV positive. I was wrong all of these years. I am so sorry. I can't do this. Please don't leave me."

"I'm not going anywhere." Carol said confidently.

"Carol, please." Byron was crying uncontrollably.

Carol watched. She wished she had something wonderful to say to relieve his pain, but it seemed greater than she had ever imagined. "Byron," she said gently. "You've apologized to me already. I'm done and passed all of that old shit. There's really no need for this."

"Yes there is," he blurted out.

"What is it, Byron? What do you want?"

"Forgiveness." He sniffled.

"Oh God, Byron, of course I forgive you. I forgave you a long time ago. You're my brother-in-law. I love you. I forgive you. Everything is okay."

Byron's tear filled eyes met Carol's. "Thank you."

"You're welcome."

Byron swallowed hard. "Please be strong. Be careful in surgery and don't let us lose you," he begged.

" Just for you," Carol smiled. "I promise."

"Carol." The distant voice was weak, but familiar.

Carol looked around. All she saw was white, it wasn't even a room. She was surrounded by the color white. "This is it? This is Heaven? Pretty boring," she said to herself.

Suddenly a figure appeared and walked towards her. The silhouette was fuzzy, but as the person approached Carol could see the figure was a man.

"Carol." He spoke again. His voice was soft and memorable, but she couldn't remember where she had heard the voice before.

He came into the light. Carol gasped when she saw his face. It was her father, Walter.

"Dad?" Carol cried out weakly. She ran over to him, but stopped herself from embracing him. "Wait. What is this? Where am I? You look the same, Dad, even after all these years. What's going on?"

"I'm here to prepare you." He spoke without emotion.

"Prepare me? For what?"

"You're smart, kiddo. You know what's coming. You need to make sure everything is in order."

The meaning of Walter's cryptic words became clear to Carol. Fear and confusion enveloped her. She couldn't make sense of anything. She had wanted to see her father again for so long, but she didn't want it to be under these circumstances. Her heart began to race. Her breathing became shallow. Was this really the end? She didn't know. Could he really tell the future? Carol focused on her breathing and tried to calm herself. "But everything wasn't in order when you left, Dad. Nothing was in order, it was all out of order. Mom and I..." Carol let her thoughts end there. She was angry, but she couldn't be mad at her father.

"It was, kiddo. Everything was in order in my heart." Walter stood motionless.

"I don't understand."

"Carol, it was very messy that night; you're right. But I knew how bright and resilient you were. I knew you'd make it. I knew that you would be okay. I had all the faith in the world in you that you would overcome your mother's harsh words and that you would build a good life for yourself. And you did. You made me so proud.

"Even that night, I was proud of you. I knew that wasn't easy to tell us. But, I loved you no matter what. Coming out that night didn't change that. When I was out on my bike, I realized that I couldn't stay married to someone who couldn't love my daughter for all that she was. I was going to go home that night and end it with your mother. But instead, I was hit."

"You were going to divorce Mom?" Carol's voiced trembled.

"Yes," Walter replied gently. "Your mother harbored a lot of anger, kiddo, even from long before you were born. She just turned into a very bitter person. She was no longer wounded and vulnerable like she was when I first met her. She became belligerent. I couldn't stay with someone like that and I knew she was cruel to you as well. My death actually spared you from years of more heartache from her."

Carol was stunned by her father's words.

"Carol, I'm sorry. We don't have much time. I really need you to listen to me.

"I am extremely proud of you. You did very well for yourself. You used your brain to get far in life. You own a successful company. You made me so proud. You did well. Really well, kiddo.

"I love Alex," Walter continued. "She is a wonderful person. I don't care about her color or gender. She loves you and took good care of you. She's an excellent daughter-in-law. Again, you've made me very proud."

He paused for a moment before continuing on. "Don't

worry about your mother. You won't hear from her. Don't let that silence get to you. You've done so well on your own. It's time to just focus on you. You've always given do much to others. It's time for you now."

He shook his head ruefully. "I am so sorry you got AIDS from the transfusion. I was the one who pushed for it back then. Had I known, I would have done something different. I'd do anything to save my little girl, but ... I'm sorry. From the depths of my soul, I am sorry, Carol."

Walter paused, transfixed on the image of his daughter. "Oh, I know you've always wondered." Walter's tone changed. "Greg Dawson called you 'kid' because of me. I made sure that you went to work with him. He was a good man, wasn't he? I grew up with him. I wanted to be sure your career was in good hands. Greg didn't realize the connection, but that wouldn't have mattered anyway. I wanted you to hear 'kid' or 'kiddo' so you knew I wasn't gone. I put a bug in his ear so that he called you 'kid.'" Walter smiled at his beautiful daughter.

"Alex's family loves you. You taught them all how to truly love and accept others. You did more for that family than you will ever know. Just make sure that you show them how much they mean to you before you go."

"How?" Carol asked.

"Through your words and actions, sweetheart. Tell them how you feel. Do something to show them that you love them."

Carol thought about her father's words. He was always so wise. She knew that he was giving her the most important advice of her life. After a pause, she asked, "How about the car?"

"Ah, the GTO. Our family car. Best purchase I ever made, huh? Remember, you can't take it with you, kiddo. Do what you think is right. I know you'll figure out a way to keep Alex's family happy. I'm thrilled we both got to enjoy it. It is a great car, isn't it?"

"Yeah," Carol whispered. A weak smile formed on her lips.

Walter sighed. "I need to leave you now, Carol. Just know that I love you and I'll see you again very soon. You have nothing to fear. Take my words and hold on to them until I see you again. I love you. It's going to be okay, kiddo."

"I love you, Dad." Carol's voice cracked as her father faded from view.

"How do you feel about your surgery tomorrow?" Dr. Parker asked.

"Good. I've been waiting for this for so long," Carol replied brightly.

"I'm glad that you're optimistic about things. Are you nervous?"

Carol paused to think. "No. Not really. I know there's always a risk with surgery, but this has to happen. I don't want to wait any more."

"Fair enough," Dr. Parker said. "What are you going to think about before the surgery?"

"Huh?"

Dr. Parker explained, "A lot of people like to think about happy memories, vacation spots and the like right before they go in for surgery. What about you? Any particular vacation spots you really liked, or...?"

"We never went on vacation."

"Really?" Dr. Parker couldn't mask his surprise. "Why is that?"

"As a kid, we couldn't really do anything because of my medical expenses. My parents couldn't even afford for me to get braces, which is why I still have this damn gap in my teeth, so traveling was definitely out of the question."

"When I became an adult, I still had this notion that vacations were only for the rich. Alex and I wanted to travel, but we were so busy with work. And we liked having some extra money that we could donate to HRC or AIDS research or greyhound rescue. Ours was a comfortable life. We were happy with what we had and what we did."

"Was there any one place you both really felt drawn to?"

Carol paused to think. "Yeah," she lightly chuckled after a minute. "We discussed going to Canada to get married right after Byron's wedding. It would have been the first international trip for both of us. We thought it would be fun and romantic. We just never got that opportunity."

"Canada is beautiful." Dr. Parker said with great enthusiasm. "I think you'd like it there, Carol. There is such a wide variety of things to see and do. From horseback riding to history. I could see you being very happy there. Plus, there's the opportunity for same sex couples to be legally married. I know that would have meant a lot to you."

"Yeah," Carol whispered.

"I think you have your vacation spot." Dr. Parker said gently. "Think about Canada tomorrow. Think of all the sights and experiences you could have. Think about being able to marry the woman you love. Focus on all of that tomorrow and you'll do well, Carol."

Carol smiled up at Dr. Parker. "I will. Thanks."

Shelby walked into Carol's room. Carol turned her head and looked at her.

"Wow, Carol. You have a line of visitors here to see you."

"Send them in, Shelby." Carol replied weakly.

"They said they wanted to come in one at a time."

"Okay. That's fine. Whatever."

"Are you up to having visitors?"

"Yeah, I think so."

"Okay," Shelby's eyes smiled at Carol. She turned and left the room.

After a few silent moments, Candace waddled into the room.

"Hey," Carol said.

"Hey," Candace exhaled. "At least they were nice enough to let me go first. Since I'm gonna have this baby any minute, I needed to get first dibs."

Carol chuckled.

"Carol, no matter where I am, no matter what is going on, I'm praying for you. I pray that the surgery goes well and that it is the first step towards real healing for you. I may not be here, but I will be with you in spirit. I know that you will do well and that everything will turn out as it should. I may be in labor while you're in there, but I'll still be praying for you." Candace's smile reached her eyes.

"Thanks," Carol smiled back.

"I have to tell you, girl, you are something special."

"How's that?" Carol asked.

"You should see the group of people out there to see you. It's crazy. It's awesome, actually. We are such a diversified group and you brought all these different people together. We all share one amazing thing in common, you. It's really quite incredible." Candace winked at her.

"Wow. That's the sweetest thing anyone has ever said to me. Thank you, C." Carol smiled brightly.

Candace reached her hand out and gently held Carol's

hand with her own gloved hand. “I love you, Carol. Don’t you ever forget that.” Her voice was peaceful and sweet.

“I won’t. I love you too.”

“I need to get my pregnant ass back to a bench out there. I’ll see you later.”

“Okay.” Carol smiled as she watched Candace slowly waddle from the room.

Shortly after Candace left, Tyrone came in.

“Hey Tyrone.” Carol greeted him.

“Hiya Carol. I have to take Candace home, so I have to...”

“I understand, Tyrone.” Carol smiled at him.

“Carol, I really wanted to thank you for everything. Isaac is doing well because of you. He’s studying computers and all kinds of crazy technological stuff. Stuff that I can’t even understand. You inspired him, Carol. On behalf of him, and my entire family, I thank you.”

“I also wanted to thank you for being such a positive person in this family. You walked into a mine field when you first met everyone, but you stayed strong. You were true to yourself and to Alex. You’ve really been a role model to all of us.”

“Wow. Thank you, Tyrone. That’s so sweet.”

“It’s true, Carol. Remember that when you go under tomorrow, okay?”

“I will, Tyrone. Thank you.”

“You’re welcome. I better get Candace home now.”

“Yeah.” Carol nodded understandingly.

Tyrone took a last look at Carol before he left.

Carol waited for the next visitor. Will came in.

“Will, you’re here!”

"Of course, Carol. I had to visit my boss."

"Former boss," Carol lightly corrected him.

"Former or not, you're still my friend. I couldn't let you go into surgery without letting you know how much I love you."

"Awe, Will. Thank you."

"You're an incredible woman, Carol. You've remained strong in the face of so much adversity. You've done so incredibly well for yourself. You're a real fighter. I can't wait till you can get out of here and get back to work."

Carol laughed. "I'll do my best, new boss."

Will chuckled. "I won't work you too hard. Seriously, I need your help on the business end of things. Just get better soon, ok?"

"I will." Carol smiled up at him.

"Thanks, boss." Will was clearly smiling under his surgical mask. "Love you, Carol."

"I love you too, Will. I'll see you when I get out."

Will swallowed hard. "Yeah." He said, choking back tears. "See you later." He quickly turned and left so Carol wouldn't see him cry.

Carol took a deep breath and waited.

"Hey girl." Robyn shouted before she could even be seen.

"Hey Robyn. How are you?" Carol's voice sounded weaker. These visits were taking a lot out of her.

"I'm good. I have this for you," she said extending a bag full of folded papers. Aware that Carol was unable to grab onto the bag, she placed it on the floor next to Carol's bed.

"What is this?" Carol asked.

"These are all get well cards from my class. I told them that a very nice person was in the hospital and they wanted to do something for you."

"Aww, that is so sweet. Thank you, Robyn."

"You're welcome, Carol. Stay strong. I know you can get through this. You've been through much worse."

Carol smiled. "I'll do my best."

"You kick some serious medical butt tomorrow, you understand?" Robyn laughed.

"Yes ma'am." Carol laughed with her.

"Good. Take care, Carol. Will and I will see you when you're out."

"Okay. Bye, Robyn." Carol still smiled as she watched Robyn walk away.

Dave came in almost immediately after Robyn left.

"Hey Dave." Carol yawned.

"Hi Carol. I just wanted you to know that John and I love you, and we can't wait for you to get out of this hell hole."

"You and me both, Dave." Carol chuckled.

"I know. May this surgery get you back on track and home soon."

"Thank you, Dave. I appreciate it." Carol's voice was soft. She felt fatigued, but she loved every minute of these visits.

"You're welcome. Get better quickly."

"I will."

Without saying another word, Dave left the room. She heard the door shut behind him, no one came in. Several moments passed before the door re-opened.

John entered Carol's room quietly. "Hey Carol."

"Hi John," she replied tiredly. "How are you?"

"I'm fine. Just wanting to see my dear friend get well

soon and finally go home."

"That would be nice. But even after this surgery, I'll be in here for weeks doing physical therapy and stuff."

"I know. Hopefully it will go easy and you'll be home before you know it."

"It would be nice to be back in the house, to see Sugar again. To have what little remains of my life back. Anything is better than this place." Carol lightly laughed.

"Yeah." John nodded in complete understanding. "Dave and I will be here when you get out of surgery."

"Okay, John. Thanks." Carol summoned the strength to smile brightly at John.

"Take care, Carol." John said sweetly. He smiled at her and slowly left the room.

Erin entered Carol's room quietly. "Hey," she said softly.

"Hi Erin." Carol's exhaustion was undeniable now.

"How are you feeling?"

"Tired. And like I'm about to have major surgery to screw and pin bones back together. Kind of crazy, huh?"

"Yeah," Erin replied. "It's not going to be an easy road from here, Carol. Recovery from a surgery like this is hard on any patient, but it's magnified tenfold for AIDS patients. You have to be brave and diligent, Carol. If there is anyone who can do it, it's you. You're strong and incredibly resilient. Just focus on what's most important and you'll be out of here before you know it."

"Yeah. Thanks, Erin. You're the first one who didn't sugar coat it for me. I appreciate that. Thank you."

"You are welcome. I've seen too much in my career. And I know you. There's no need to lie to you. You're tough. You can handle it. I admire that about you, Carol."

" Thank you, Erin. That really means a lot to me. Thank

you so much."

"You're welcome. Take good care of yourself."

"You got it," Carol smiled at Erin.

Erin smiled back at Carol for a minute before she finally exited the room.

Carol fought to keep her eyes open. She adored her friends and family and these visits meant the world to her. Her body was tired and fatigued. She hoped that she'd be able to rest soon.

"Hey." The voice was deep and familiar. Byron walked in slowly.

"Hi, B. How are you? Feeling better since we last talked?"

"Yeah." Byron was already fighting tears. "I love you Carol. We all love you."

"I love you too, Byron. I love all of you. I couldn't have asked for better people in my life."

"That's because you're one of the greatest people in our lives, Carol."

"Thanks, Byron."

Tears began escaping Byron's dark brown eyes. "You stay strong. Remember your promise to me."

"How could I forget?" Carol smiled up at him. "I wouldn't make a promise I couldn't keep."

"Okay. I'll see you when you get out?" He sniffled.

"Yeah," Carol said gently.

"Okay. Good night, Carol. I love you."

"I love you too, B."

Byron quickly turned and left the room. He was unable to fight his tears any more.

Carol sighed a deep sigh. She loved her family. She adored their kind words. She wished they could surround her at all times. For now, she needed to be strong and face this coming day alone. She closed her eyes and allowed her weary body to get the rest it so desperately needed.

"Okay, Carol. Are you ready?" Shelby asked after Carol was moved to a gurney. All of Carol's various lines and monitors were switched to a portable IV poles. Carol was already wearing a mask and other protective gear. This was the first time she would be out of her hospital room. She was both excited and nervous.

"Yeah, I'm ready." She said as stoically as she could.

"Alright. Let's go." Shelby said. She and another nurse mastered all of the various rolling poles, machines and the gurney as they traveled the hospital hallway towards the surgical area. Carol tried to study what she could of the hall. It was nice having a change of scenery. Carol didn't want to forget these sights, she knew it would be a long time before she saw them again.

They made their way to the surgical suite. Two more nurses were waiting for them, and helped Shelby and the first nurse to set up all of Carol's equipment. After all of the machines and lines were set up, the team gently moved Carol from the gurney onto the surgical table.

Another unknown masked face approached Carol. "Hi Ms. Mathers. My name is Dr. Young. I will be your anesthesiologist for today."

"Okay," Carol nervously replied.

I am going to inject a medication. You might feel something warm going through your vein for a minute. Then, I'm going to place a mask over your face and have you count backwards from ten. Okay?"

“Yeah.” Carol’s fear was mounting.

“I know this is scary, but you’ll be fine.” Dr. Young said as he slowly pushed a white liquid medication into one of Carol’s IV lines. She felt the warmth he was describing.

Dr. Young grabbed a face mask. Quickly, he pulled off her surgical mask and placed the mask over her face. “Okay. Can you count backwards from ten for me?”

“Ten,” Carol said weakly. “Nine... eight.” Her words became slurred. The room was melting away. “Seven... six.” Darkness swept over Carol and she was in a deep sleep.

Chapter 19

“Hey Byron. Can you go reach that brief case for me? There’s something I need to show you.” Carol felt so weak she could barely move her head. Byron looked down at her. Carol wasn’t even recognizable. She was gaunt. Her eyes were sunken. Her skin was pale and the whites of her eyes were a haunting pale yellow. There was a huge metal contraption keeping her legs and pelvis in a fixed position. This was not the vibrant, intelligent woman he once knew.

Byron reached down to the brief case and opened it. There was one lone paper in it, with keys lying on top.

“I need the paper first,” Carol said weakly.

He grabbed it and handed it to Carol.

“Byron,” Carol said as she weakly grasped the paper. “This is the title to the GTO.”

There was confusion in Byron’s deep, dark eyes.

“I have no need for it. It’s not practical for Tyrone and Candace. Besides, you were the one who purchased it. My father’s memory deserves to live on and you should enjoy the car.” Carol held a pen in her debilitated grasp and scribbled her signature on the title.

Byron looked at the paper as Carol handed it back to him and sighed heavily. “Carol...”

“Byron, don’t say anything.”

“But I can’t.”

“Why not? You gave this to me as a gift, now I am giving it to you as a gift. Take it.” She paused to look at the keys. “Do you see those two smaller keys?”

“Yes,” Byron said, there was a catch in his voice.

“Those are the keys to the GTO. Those are yours. The

other keys are the keys to the house. Candace needs to get those."

"What?" Byron was in shock.

"Candace is getting the house. She and the baby will be well cared for. Alex and I made sure of that a while ago. You don't need to worry about them."

Byron was in awe.

"As for you, I can't let the GTO rot away. You bought this car for me. Your sister and I enjoyed it for years. Now it's your turn. What you do with it after I'm gone is up to you. But I have to sign it over to you. I need to do this before I die."

"Carol, please don't talk like that." Byron's voice cracked.

"I'm sorry, Byron. I know this is hard, but it's true."

Again, Byron sighed heavily as he fought back the tears. "Okay, Carol.." With the signed title and keys in his hand, Byron left the room. He was unable to look at Carol any longer.

"I did it, Dad." Carol feebly whispered, hoping that her father could hear her.

Carol repeatedly pressed the call button. It seemed like an eternity before a nurse finally came in. Carol could hardly speak. She feared that opening her mouth might cause her to vomit again, as she had been doing most of the night.

"Have you thrown up again?" The nurse sounded concerned.

"No," Carol replied weakly.

"What can I do for you then?" The nurse's voice was soft and gentle.

"I, I can't take this pain," Carol grunted.

"Pain? Hold on. Let me get Dr. Ramone in here." The nurse left quickly.

Carol felt consumed by pain.

After a few moments, Dr. Ramone came in with the nurse right behind him. "What's wrong, Carol?"

“I can’t take this pain. It’s fucking awful. Oh God, it hurts.”

“She’s been vomiting for hours,” the nurse whispered to Dr. Ramone.

“Pain?” He asked Carol, ignoring the nurse. “What kind of pain? Where does it hurt?”

“I... hurt... everywhere.” Carol gasped between every word.

“Where is it worst?”

“My stomach,” Carol replied weakly.

Dr. Ramone looked at Carol’s yellow hue. Gently, he palpated Carol’s abdomen. As he did she screamed out in pain. Her voice echoed off the hospital walls. Dr. Ramone turned to the nurse. “I want a full panel run on her stat. Give her a bolus of fluids to re-hydrate her and an extra dose of pain meds. Call me immediately when the results come back.”

“Yes, Dr. Ramone.” The nurse said and promptly left the room.

“It’s going to be ok, Carol. Just hang in there and we’ll get you comfortable again.” Dr. Ramone said as he held her hand. She tried to squeeze his large hand to focus her mind away from the pain. Carol’s face was contorted from the pain. He knew this was bad. He hoped that the medicine would bring her relief and that the blood work wouldn’t be as horrific as he suspected. After a few silent moments, Dr. Ramone left.

Carol continued to breathe hard, she grunted as she waited for the nurse to come back with something to relieve her pain.

Byron, Candace, Tyrone and Erin stood around Carol’s bed. She didn’t move. Her eyes were closed. Her EKG monitor beeped quietly in the background.

“Her organ function has decreased significantly,” Dr. Ramone informed them. “It’s extremely painful at this stage, so we have her heavily sedated. It’s the best we can do for her until she passes.”

Everyone looked at him at the same time. They were

stunned by his words. They knew that Carol had taken a risk to have the surgery, but they didn't realize how close her death was.

"I'm sorry. This is all we can do for now." The doctor took Carol's chart and walked out of the room. The family remained in the room in silence.

Tyrone sat with Carol in her room. She slept. Carol hadn't been conscious in days. Each of the family members took turns staying with her. It was silent torture.

"There's no quality of life." He murmured as looked over at her bed. Carol's skin was a sickening shade of yellow. Her breaths were weak and shallow. There was no life left in her. She was simply a sedated body, waiting to exit the Earth. Tyrone sighed. "She has no life, really Lord, please take her soon." Tyrone gently prayed.

Candace was reading as Carol continued to silently lie in her bed. Suddenly, Candace felt a great pressure; it seemed to consume her entire body. Candace doubled over in pain. She took a few deep breaths and it subsided. She looked up. Carol's monitors were different. Candace's eyes scanned the various machines until she found the culprit. Carol's heart rate had increased.

Candace carefully pushed herself up to take a closer look at Carol's vital signs when she felt that tremendous pain again. Candace quickly sat back in the chair. She focused on her breathing until the pain dissipated. Once the pain had eased, Candace picked up her head and slowly stood again to look at Carol's monitors. As she did so, another massive wave of pain came over her and warm liquid ran down her legs. Shocked, Candace looked down at the floor. Her water had broken, she was in labor. Thinking quickly, Candace grabbed the handle and pressed the button to call a nurse. She forgot the reason she stood up in the first place. Her mind was solely focused on her baby now. Carol's heart rate continued to increase, unnoticed.

A nurse ran in. "What's wrong, Ms. Whetherby?"

"My water just broke," Candace said. She sounded scared. The nurse left and quickly returned with a wheelchair. She gently helped Candace into the wheelchair and hurriedly moved Candace to labor and delivery.

Alone in her room, Carol's heart rate continued to speed up.

Later that afternoon, Byron watched over Carol as she lay in her bed. The EKG monitor beeped softly in the background. "I'm sorry, Carol." He whispered in the hopes that she might hear it before she passed. "You are a far greater person than you ever knew. We all love you." Tears welled up in his eyes. He watched her in silence. Sometimes her heart rate seemed very high, other times it was frighteningly slow.

Carol's heart rate became increasingly sporadic until it finally stopped all together.

Hearing the machine drone, Byron looked around the room in a panic. "Somebody get in here!" His large voice echoed through the hospital hallways.

A doctor and two nurses rushed in. Carol's heart had finally given up. The doctor approached Carol diminutive body. He quickly felt for pulses, listened for a heart beat and checked for any signs of life. After a minute, the doctor walked over to Byron. "I'm sorry, sir. She's gone. There's nothing more we could have done for her."

"No! Give her something! My wife is a nurse. I know you can inject her with something. Save her." He screamed through his tears.

"I'm sorry, Mr. Whetherby. I can't. She's gone. There is nothing more we can do. It's over."

Byron began to wail. Tears flowed freely down his face. The nurses quickly and quietly disconnected all of Carol's various lines and machines. They silently placed a sheet over her body.

The nurses and doctor led Byron from the room. They compassionately offered sympathy. Byron couldn't hear past his own sobs.

As they walked down the hall, Dr. Anderson ran to

Byron. "Congratulations, Mr. Whetherby. You are the proud uncle of a beautiful, healthy, baby girl."

"What?" Byron said in a daze.

"Your sister delivered a little baby girl. She's awake and they're both doing well. You can go visit her, if you'd like."

Confused, Byron ran through the hospital to get to Candace.

After running down three flights of stairs and through a maze of endless halls, Byron finally reached Candace's room. Candace was sitting in her bed watching Tyrone sleep in a chair next to her.

"You had her?" Byron asked out of breath.

"Yes," Candace softly replied.

"A girl?" Byron walked over to her.

"Yep. A little girl." Candace smiled up at her big brother.

He looked down at her, unable to speak. "Carol's gone." Byron finally uttered the words.

"I know," Candace whispered. She held her brother's large hand in her own. "It was her time, B. She needed to go." Candace paused and then whispered to herself, "shine on you crazy diamond."

Byron broke down hysterically crying. "It was her birthday. And now it's your daughter's birthday."

"I know." Candace's voice was gentle and wise. "It was a fitting ending for Carol. She waited just for this."

"But she's gone. And Alex is gone. Everything is different now." Byron cried harder.

"Sssshhhh. I know, B. They are gone, but they're not forgotten. They're going to live on with us."

"How?" Byron sniffled as he wiped a tear from his large brown eyes.

"My daughter's name is Carol Alexandria Whetherby. They will both be with us."

Byron cried more. He bent over his sister. Candace carefully reached up and held her brother as he cried.

Epilogue

Candace unpacked the last suitcase. She had been so busy after having the baby and moving her new family into Carol and Alex's home. It was surreal to be in that home, knowing neither of them would ever be there again. This was now her home. Candace would make it her own while still cherishing the memories of Carol and Alex.

She reached into the suitcase and pulled out a small hard object. As she picked it up, she recognized the journal she had given to Carol in the hospital. On those pages were Carol's last thoughts, feelings, and dreams. Her entire life was somehow contained on just a few pieces of paper.

Hesitantly, Candace opened the journal and began to read the words that Carol had scribbled out. The emotions were so raw that tears began flowing from her eyes. Candace quickly closed the book and took a deep breath. She both treasured and feared this small journal.

Something stirred in Candace's heart. Without even knowing the reason why, Candace walked into the office and sat down at her computer. The painting Carol had painted in the hospital hung on the wall above the computer. After staring at it for a moment, Candace knew what she needed to do.

She began typing.

Carol had anticipated this day for years. Just like so many college students, the day she could legally drink was a great rite of passage in her life.

Marlene, Carol's roommate, along with other friends and fellow students, had planned a wild night for their typically reclusive friend. Carol knew it would be a long, unpredictable night despite her early class. Carol didn't care, though. She never went out and never partied. Her social life typically consisted of long nights with her textbooks. She deserved this one night to live it up.

At around seven, there was a thunderous pounding on Carol's dorm room door. Wearing makeup and nice clothes for a change, Carol opened the door. A herd of people stood in front of her, some of whom Carol didn't even recognize. She didn't mind. This was her night. Tonight was her night to live, to laugh, and to enjoy.

"Surprise!" Everyone shouted, but the surprise was on them. Marlene was floored to find Carol wearing an uncharacteristically soft, delicate, slightly ruffled black blouse and a cute asymmetrical black skirt. This was Marlene's first time in four years seeing Carol in anything other than a tee-shirt and jeans. Her outfit confirmed her ownership of this night. Carol grabbed her winter coat and purse and the crowd left to go paint the town.

Marlene had decided on the evening's venue. Since her roommie was openly gay, Marlene led the crowd to the best lesbian bar in town: City Girls.

Carol's troops wasted no time in splurging on shots, beer and a variety of hard alcoholic beverages. Carol, normally introverted, drank the shots and other intoxicating spirits; it didn't take long for her to become inebriated.

Alexandria, a 24-year old local, watched the loud, raucous group and quietly chuckled to herself. She went to City Girls tonight to people watch and she certainly got an eye-full.

Suddenly, Carol got off her bar stool to go to the ladies' room. Carol tripped over her own two drunken feet and began to fall forward. She saved herself by slamming her hand on the table in front of Alex. Embarrassed, Carol slowly pulled herself up to find the dark beauty smiling back at her. With skin like rich, dark chocolate, eyes that were beautiful, tranquil, bottomless pools, and neatly braided jet black hair, Alexandria took Carol's breath away. The two paused and the world around them melted away as they intensely stared at each other.

"Sorry," Carol weakly whispered. Mortified that she had made such a fool of herself in front of this stunning woman, Carol hastily stumbled to the ladies' room.

Carol leaned onto the sink and held on to it with all her might in fear she might fall over again. She took in a few deep breaths as she stared at herself in the mirror. Carol's beauty was her simplicity. She had brown hair to her shoulder in a simple style, but there was a special charm to it. Her skin was fair and delicately painted with tiny freckles. Her face seemed plain, but it was brilliantly symmetrical. The very tip of her nose turned upward in a playful manner. Her deep brown eyes sparkled like jewels. She had a slight gap in between her front teeth; Carol was embarrassed by it, but her father had always compared her to model Lauren Hutton. He told his beloved daughter that the imperfection made her unique and beautiful. Carol sighed thinking of her father's words. She pushed the faucet on for cold water and took a few handfuls to sip with the unrealistic hope she would miraculously sober up. She really wanted to go back and talk to that gorgeous mahogany queen. Focusing on her father's words telling her that she was pretty, Carol mustered up the courage to go back out and speak to the woman who currently occupied every thought in her mind.

Carol took a step slowly and then stepped again. She focused on each step and she walked back out to the bar, this time with a bit more grace.

As she turned the corner, she saw the beautiful black woman still sitting at the table. Carol's crowd hadn't even noticed her absence.

Alexandria happened to look up at just the right moment, and saw Carol carefully approaching her. Alex's dark eyes lit up and she smiled a big, beautiful, wide smile at the birthday girl.

Carol carefully sat across from the intriguing woman. "Hi," she said feebly. "I'm so sorry about before. I normally never drink, but today's my twenty first birthday."

Alex began to laugh lightly. "It's okay. I understand." Her voice was smooth and rich. Carol was becoming more intoxicated on this woman than she was on the alcohol. "I'm Alexandria. My friends call me Alex." The dark beauty extended her hand to Carol.

Carol grasped her hand. Alex's skin was soft and as smooth as silk. "I'm Carol," she replied. "My friends call me

Carol," she joked as she gently shook Alex's hand. Alex couldn't help chuckling at Carol's wisecrack.

Suddenly, a large wave of cheers and shouts sounded from the bar. Both Alex and Carol looked over. Carol's group was intently engaged in a drinking game. The team of people who had come with her were busy celebrating, having completely forgotten the cause of the celebration. They didn't appear to be slowing down either. It didn't matter though, Carol was enjoying this quiet time with Alex more than anything. Alexandria's company was an exceptional birthday present for Carol.

Alex stole a glance at her watch. "Well, it was nice meeting you."

Carol looked up at Alex, startled.

"It's 11:30 already. I need to go."

"I should go too. I have an 8 o'clock class," Carol replied.

"Do you want a ride home?" The question was unexpected. Carol wasn't sure if she should trust this woman she had just met. Whether alcohol induced, or caused by infatuation, she accepted the offer.

The two ladies quietly left City Girls and walked to Alex's white Camry. Alex opened the door for Carol. Even in her drunken state, Carol thought about A Bronx Tale, and quickly unlocked the door for Alex.

"Thanks," Alex winked as she got in. "So, where to, birthday girl?"

Carol blushed. "I live at the Martin-Haagen dorm at the University."

"Yes, ma'am," Alex enthusiastically answered. "What are you studying?"

"I'm a computer science major with a history minor."

"That's an unusual pairing."

"I know. I'd love to be an historian," Carol admitted, "but I know I'd have a better career in computers."

"Smart plan. I'm impressed."

"Thanks." Carol blushed again. "What about you?"

"I'm a paralegal."

"That's really interesting," Carol said sincerely.

"It's okay. It's a living." Alex pulled up to the front of Carol's dorm. "Well, I guess we're here."

"Oh," Carol said, surprised that the trip had seemed so quick, too quick. "Thanks." She began to open the door.

"Wait," implored Alex. Carol turned to look at the striking woman again. "Did you get what you wanted for your birthday?"

Carol paused for a moment. "Yeah, I spent my birthday with great company," she answered flirtatiously.

"How about something sweet for your special day?" Carol looked at Alex, puzzled. Alex slowly leaned in and gently kissed Carol. Her lips were warm, soft, and inviting. It was the sweetest birthday present Carol ever had. Slowly, Alex pulled away and the two women just smiled at each other. Alex took Carol's hand and placed something in it. "Here's my card," she said tantalizingly. "Feel free to call me, any time."

Carol sat in the car staring at this amazing woman. "Thanks," she quietly replied. Reluctantly, she opened the door and slowly stepped out.

"Happy birthday," Alex called through the open door. Her smile seemed endless now. Carol gleamed back as the car door closed.

Carol watched Alex pull away. This was definitely Carol's best birthday ever. She looked forward to seeing Alex again.

More Great Books by Lauren Shiro

Impeceable

Carol – abandoned - waiting… for what, she couldn't know. She couldn't see that there was more life waiting for her. Carol is forced to face the demons of her past as well as begin to face life without Alex. Struggling to make sense of it all, Carol experiences her new life and all of the highs and lows that come with that life.

Unbreakable Hostage

Lareina Oliveira; she wants to share her passion for math. So it is back to school for Lareina… a tough Ph.D. program. A classmate is captivated by Lareina's beauty and intelligence, and despite her repeated refusals to his attentions, he kidnaps her! Only her determination and wits can save her…

Loving Her, Volume 1
by Lauren Shiro

In this series of stories, we meet a group of loving friends and couples. Each member of this group is diverse in personalities and abilities, but they are tied together by the common denominator - love.

from Chelle Cordero, Combining Passion & Suspense

This volume contains the first four stories in the Loving Her series. Each is also available as individual short stories. Loving Her, Volume 1 is coming soon in audio, and is available in print and all electronic editions.

Book 1
The Ballerina

A southern, redheaded, pickup driving lesbian ballerina? You bet! Meet Liz: a southern belle with flair. Vivacious, eclectic and graceful, she is unique to say the least. The first in the series of Loving Her stories, Liz's story is the kind that stays with you long after you've closed the book.

Book 2
The Cop

Donna White is one tough cop. Behind the badge, though, is a very sweet, sad, sensitive soul. Truly a woman alone, Donna is simply trying to navigate her way through life. Who is Donna? She is dedicated, determined, distinctive and deep. Donna's rich and touching story is second in the Loving Her series.

Book 3
The Mechanic

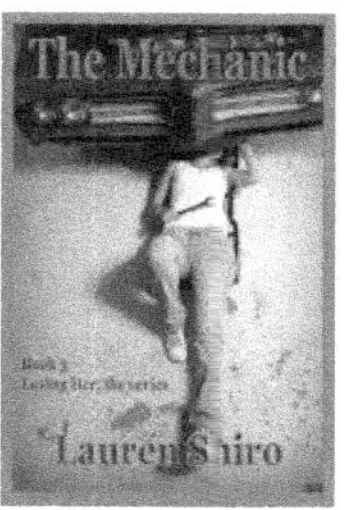

Linda - her name means beautiful... After facing rejection from her parents because she is a lesbian, Linda didn't feel beautiful... she felt lost and alone. As a skilled mechanic, Linda built her business... Her love life was a different matter. Until Katie... They survived the brutal beatings they received at the hands of Katie's ultra-religious father. Together they survived, and together would face their future, and find hope and a joy neither expected.

Book 4
The Model

She's exotic. She's beautiful. She's talented. She's unique. She's Stephania. A young successful model who started from nothing, she has experienced all the ups and downs of life. Never one to be kept down, she persists through life's trials and reaches for the fairytale ending she has always hoped for. Stephania's emotional journey is the fourth story in the Loving Her series.

Book 5
The Peace Officer

Brynn Racanelli - daughter, sister, friend, partner, police officer... and so much more. Devoted to serving others through her police work, and to helping her sister who battles chronic Lyme Disease, she is the the poster child of selflessness. But she does have wants, needs, hopes, and dreams. Will fate finally bring her the life and love she's always dreamed of?

Book 6
The Shelter Director

Shy, quiet, humble – Jen is the kind of person that would give you the shirt off her back and then ask you what else you need. She may not be a movie star, but she'll treat you like one. She works diligently to help save cats. She sacrifices her life and stability to accommodate her partner. She gives until it hurts, and her reward is a devastating diagnosis. What will her life become?

Book 7
The Writer

Everyone has that one friend; the mother of the group. Maria is that one friend; nurturing, wise, and with a spicy streak, Maria is the matriarch of the clan. Cerebral, emotional, and even sometimes comical, Maria's story is the seventh in the Loving Her series.

Book 8
The Vet Student

Determined to escape the small town and her religious, stifling parents,Katie works hard to get into veterinary school... in Philadelphia. Katie refused to let anything – or anyone – destroy her dream. Not even her own parents. She suffered many losses along the way, but she gained so much more. Tumultuous and tender, Katie's story closes the Loving Her series... for now.

Amnesie, a short story

What happens to love when life changes? Two women in love, one debilitating change...

Trajectory, a short story

Joe Davis has spent the last four years of his life behind a scope as a sniper for the Detroit PD's SWAT Team. A fateful call sends Joe and his team deep into the Detroit Ghetto; and reminds him that there is more to life than what's on the other end of his gun.

Lauren Shiro

Love without Boundaries

In celebration of her one year wedding anniversary and recent political changes that legalize her marriage, author Lauren E. Harvey (L. E. Harvey) and Vanilla Heart Publishing are excited to announce the re-releases of her books and a brand new series of Loving Her singles under her (legal) married name, Lauren Shiro.

Lauren Shiro was published nationally for the first time at age fourteen. Since then, her work has been published in newspapers, magazines, literary journals, and even textbooks.

In 2006, she began writing fiction and she hasn't stopped yet. From her set of intertwined short stories in *Loving Her*, to the powerhouse duo of *Imperfect* and *Impeccable*, Lauren has written stories that are sure to touch your heart. Lauren continues to write stories of love without boundaries.

When she's not writing, Lauren works as a licensed veterinary technician. In her spare time, she enjoys everything from wood working to roller derby. She resides in Rochester, New York with her wife and their menagerie of furry and feathered friends.

Visit with Lauren

Email AuthorLaurenShiro@gmail.com
Facebook Facebook.com/LaurenShiro77
Twitter twitter.com/AuthorLShiro @authorlshiro
Blog LaurenShiro.blogspot.com
Website LaurenShiro.com

www.ingramcontent.com/pod-product-compliance
Lightning Source LLC
Chambersburg PA
CBHW070850120626
46556CB00002B/944

* 9 7 8 0 6 9 2 2 3 2 5 2 1 *